Readers L[...]

T0014600

Paint by Number

"This story, like most of Andrew's books is sweet and full of feelings… If you've never read a book from Andrew Grey and even if you have, I highly recommend this one."

—Open Skye Book Reviews

"There is a saying that you can never go home again but this story will prove an exception to that."

—Paranormal Romance Guild

Hard Road Back

"I urge you to grab a copy of *Hard Road Back* so you too can discover and enjoy Martin and Scarborough's world."

—Love Bytes

Catch of a Lifetime

"…a salute to Mr. Grey's mastery of gay locution, which added enormously to my reading pleasure."

—Rainbow Book Reviews

Twice Baked

"This a great second chance romance novel… There is loads of charm and romance."

—MM Good Book Reviews

"A fun and flirty story I enjoyed and I believe you will, too."

—Bayou Book Junkie

By Andrew Grey

Published by DREAMSPINNER PRESS
www.dreamspinnerpress.com

By ANDREW GREY (cont'd)

Published by DREAMSPINNER PRESS
www.dreamspinnerpress.com

Published by DREAMSPINNER PRESS
www.dreamspinnerpress.com

ANDREW GREY

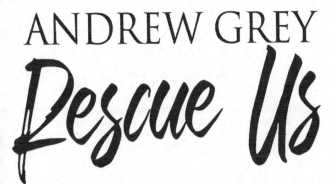

Rescue Us

DREAMSPINNER
PRESS

Published by
DREAMSPINNER PRESS

5032 Capital Circle SW, Suite 2, PMB# 279,
Tallahassee, FL 32305-7886 USA
www.dreamspinnerpress.com

This is a work of fiction. Names, characters, places, and incidents either
are the product of author imagination or are used fictitiously, and any
resemblance to actual persons, living or dead, business establishments,
events, or locales is entirely coincidental.

Rescue Us
© 2023 Andrew Grey

Cover Art
© 2023 L.C. Chase
http://www.lcchase.com
Cover content is for illustrative purposes only and any person depicted
on the cover is a model.

Mass Market Paperback ISBN: 978-1-64108-401-7
Trade Paperback ISBN: 978-1-64108-400-0
Digital ISBN: 978-1-64108-399-7
Mass Market Paperback published July 2023
v. 1.0

Printed in the United States of America

This paper meets the requirements of
ANSI/NISO Z39.48-1992 (Permanence of Paper).

To Dominic, for everything he does.

Chapter 1

"WEST CARLISLE Clinic. May I help you?" vet tech Daniel said, answering the clinic phone. Mitchell, the head vet and owner of the clinic, was in the back, trying to soothe a particularly unhappy cat after surgery. Mitchell had a way with all the animals, and Daniel could only hope he'd be just as good when he graduated. He still had a way to go, but he knew what he wanted to do with his life.

"Can I speak with Mitchell, please?" asked a man with a deep, sexy voice.

Daniel pulled himself out his momentary daydream and back to reality. "He's in the back with a patient. Can I give him a message?" He pulled out a notepad to write down the message. He'd text Mitchell once he got off the phone.

"This is Officer Van der Wall from the Shippensburg police."

"Hank?" Daniel asked with a smile. "It's Daniel Jackson. You were in the dorm room across from me in my freshman year." Daniel was surprised he hadn't recognized Hank's voice. They'd been friends a few years ago, when Hank, a senior, had helped Daniel adjust to college life.

"I remember," he said, more cheerful now than he'd been a few seconds ago. Then Hank cleared his throat. "I wish I was calling under better circumstances."

"How can I help?" Daniel shifted into professional mode.

"We have a real situation down here. An older man fell down the stairs of his home and had to be taken to the hospital. The EMTs called us because the house and yard are full of animals that need attention. The city has declared the house a hazard and ordered us to either send the animals to a shelter or have them put down. Some of them are sick, and there are a few we don't know what to do with." He sounded a little freaked out.

"Okay. Can you give me details? I'm pretty sure Mitchell has room in his shelter for some dogs." His heart suddenly beat a little faster as the instinct to help kicked in. Daniel had a connection with animals, and it hurt him to know that these ones had been left in such a vulnerable situation. When he'd been younger, he had always felt like a disappointment to his family. But animals didn't judge—they only wanted care and love, and Daniel had been happy to give it.

He'd wanted to be a vet for as long as he could remember. And he was getting there—he just needed to get accepted into a program.

"There's more than that. Let me give you a rundown for him. We have six dogs, three of which are sick and will need care, two snakes, a tortoise, and a tiger."

Daniel paused, making sure he heard that right. "Did you say a tiger?" Holy hell.

"Yes. A tiger. It's in a cage in the backyard. We don't know what to do with the exotic animals either. Mitchell was the first person I thought of." He sounded more than a little wigged now, and Daniel wondered just how close his friend had come to some of them. Still, his mind went to the tiger. The poor animal. How confused it must feel.

"Is that all?" Daniel asked. Just then, Mitchell came out front. "Hold on just a minute, Hank." Daniel put the call on hold. "Shippensburg police have a situation. Six dogs, two snakes, a tortoise, and a tiger in a home in the city. They need to find a place for them."

Mitchell nodded. "Tell them we can take the dogs, but the rest are beyond our capabilities."

Daniel lowered his gaze. "They're going to kill them if someone doesn't take them." Jesus, he needed to get himself together. "I've had reptiles as pets, so I know what to do with them. I could even take them home with me if that's necessary."

"Take them home to your apartment that only allows small dogs or cats?" Mitchell asked. He shook his head, but Daniel could already tell that he was trying to figure out what to do. And sure enough, a few minutes later, Mitchell had a plan. "Okay. The snakes and tortoise are going to need to be in terrariums and kept warm. I think we can figure something out for them. But a tiger...." He rubbed his forehead even as he picked up the phone.

Mitchell talked to Hank for a few minutes, but he did more listening than anything else. "Okay. We'll be down just as soon as the clinic closes. Two hours tops. In the meantime, I'll get things ready." He paused and then hung up the phone.

"What do you want me to do?" Daniel asked.

"You remember that break room we used to have? Well, clean it up and get it ready for three new inhabitants. I'm told there are already tanks and equipment at the house for the snakes and tortoise. They should be fine in there." He started pacing. "The city says the whole place needs to be cleaned out. The house is going to be condemned. The dogs we can house in the isolation ward of the shelter. The tiger...." He sighed. "I don't know. The officer said he thought the cat was sick, but I'll have to judge when we get there."

"We?" Daniel was so excited, he could barely stand it.

"Yes," Mitchell said. "So get busy. We leave in an hour, and I have appointments up until then. Watch the front and get the break room ready for some new friends."

Mitchell met the next patient to come through the doors, and Daniel did as he was told, listening for the phone as he pushed one of the tables against the wall and moved the microwave to the other side the room. He dug out a power strip and plugged it into the sole outlet so they could add lamps for heat. Then, after a quick look around to be sure there was enough space, he went back out front. Mitchell had just finished with his last patient and was locking the front door and flipping the sign to closed.

"The room is all set," Daniel reported, anxious to get going.

Mitchell called his husband, Beau, to let him know what was happening, while Daniel checked that all the animals in recovery were settled. Once the office was closed up for the night, he followed Mitchell out to the van for the ride to the shelter Mitchell had built by his home.

Once they got there, Beau came out to meet them with their daughter, Jessica, in his arms.

For a second, a stab of jealously raced through Daniel. Not that he had a thing for Beau. Anyone could see that Mitchell and Beau were head over heels for each other. But he did desperately want what they had. Considering the steady string of losers in his past, romance probably wasn't in the cards for him… at least right now. Although he did have a boyfriend at the moment, things weren't working out. Daniel knew he needed to break things off with Yan, but he was a little afraid to. Yan had a temper and tended to lash out when he was upset.

"How long will you be gone?" Beau asked, shifting Jessica from one hip to the other.

"I'm not sure," Mitchell said. "Hopefully not more than two hours, but I'll call you when we're on our way back."

"I'll make some dinner and have it ready when you get here." Beau leaned in to give Mitchell a quick kiss. Then Jessica, who wasn't about to be left out, slipped into Mitchell's arms for a hug and a kiss as well.

"Thank you."

Mitchell walked into the shelter while Daniel loaded the van with everything he thought they'd need—carriers, muzzles, leashes—as well as blankets to protect the tanks. By the time he was ready, Mitchell had joined him, and after waving to Beau and Jessica, they headed out.

"Are you ready for this?" Mitchell asked. "These situations can be pretty heartbreaking. The house will be filthy, and the animals will be in rough shape. But all we need to focus on is getting them out of there. I can look after them once we get back to the clinic." He frowned. "But I'm still not sure what we're going to do with the tiger. I'm not equipped to look after a cat that big." He accelerated, and Daniel made sure his seat belt was well fastened.

"Then what will they do?" Daniel asked.

Mitchell sighed. "I don't really know. It takes a lot to handle an animal like that. They aren't pets. Tigers are wild animals, and they need to be treated that way. They need a place to run and space to hunt."

Daniel bit his lower lip as he watched out the window. He knew he was getting too emotional over an animal he hadn't even met, but somehow he just knew they couldn't allow the tiger to be euthanized.

They rode for about twenty minutes before pulling into the drive of a suburban ranch house that looked like it had once been painted white but was now mostly yellowed and peeling. Mitchell came to a stop next to a police car. Hank got out and introduced himself to Mitchell, and Daniel shook his hand as well, seeing a slightly older version of the guy he'd gone to school with. He couldn't help wishing he had done a better job of keeping in touch.

"Come on. You may as well see what we're dealing with," Hank said.

"Are the dogs friendly?" Mitchell asked.

"Oh, yes. They all want attention," Hank answered.

"Then let's get them out of the house first. That way they can settle. Then we'll get the others," Mitchell said as he walked inside, with Daniel and Hank following.

Three dogs came right up to Daniel, jumping and begging for attention. Daniel attached leashes to their collars and led them outside, where he gave them plenty of scratches and love before placing each one in a carrier with some food. It broke his heart that they had been living in a place that burned his nose just by being inside for a few minutes.

When the first three dogs were settled, he steeled himself and went after the other three. They weren't as energetic, but they came easily. Outside, they lay down in the carriers as though they were exhausted. They didn't look that old, but they sure acted it. He gave them scratches and care as well, trying to reassure them that everything was going to be okay. Hopefully Mitchell could figure out what was wrong with them.

"Daniel," Mitchell called out.

Daniel secured the dogs in the back of the large van, then came around to where Mitchell stood outside a small enclosure sitting on the concrete. A tiger lay on the bare cement, his eyes half closed.

"Have you done anything to him?" Anger warred with sadness in Daniel's heart when he saw the way this majestic creature was being kept.

Hank seemed affected by the tiger's plight as well. He shook his head slowly. "No. He's pretty much been that way since we found him. We figure that it's likely he'll have to be put down. He looks sick, and there's no one to take care of him. It isn't like we can just place him with another family. Neither can you."

Daniel gasped. "Are you kidding? A Sumatran tiger?" His mind instantly clicked that this was one of the rarest big cats in the world. He pointed, and the orange and black tiger got up on all fours and yawned wide, showing off a mouth full of impressive teeth. "Hey, boy. How are you feeling?" He looked around the cage. "When did he eat last? Do you know?" His mind instantly went to what the big cat needed.

Hank shrugged but didn't answer. Not that Daniel would have expected him to know. The entire situation made his stomach roil.

"Okay. Then before we do anything, let's get him something to eat. Is there a store nearby?" Mitchell pulled out his wallet. "The poor animal is emaciated. Hank, could you please go get some beef, preferably without bones? We'll cut it up and see if he's hungry. That could be the reason he's so listless." Mitchell sounded so confident that Hank nodded and took the money, then quickly backed out of the drive, probably anxious to get away from one of the world's top land predators.

"What are we going to do? This is a Sumatran tiger—they're endangered in the wild. We can't just let him be put down." Daniel swallowed hard. He really wanted to hurt whoever had done this to the poor animal. The tiger had obviously been mistreated, and for God knows how long. It was lucky he hadn't lashed out at anyone nearby, as hungry as he had to be.

"Get the snakes and tortoise out of the house and into the van. Then drive them carefully back. Put the dogs in the quarantine area in the barn, and get the snakes and tortoise set up in the break room."

"But what about you? And him?" Daniel asked. He really didn't want to leave, looking back at the tiger. It was lying down, panting again, its eyes without hope.

"Bring back the van and the largest steel cage we have. It should fit. Once he's knocked out, we'll transfer him into it. Then we'll take down this enclosure and rebuild it back at the rescue. That will give us a safe place to keep him until we can either find him a home at a zoo or build something larger for him." Mitchell shook his head. "I can't believe I'm going to rescue a freaking tiger. Just get going. We'll have just enough time to get this done before it gets dark."

Mitchell smiled, and Daniel got on his task. He carried out the covered aquariums with the snakes and tortoise, making sure the tops were secured. Then he climbed into the van and headed back toward Carlisle.

"WHERE THE heck are you?" Yan demanded. Daniel had called him on the way back. "You were supposed to be done with work hours ago. We have dinner with the guys tonight."

"We got an emergency call." Excitement spiked inside Daniel as the dogs in back whimpered when the van bounced. He hadn't even realized he'd sped up. "You won't believe what we found."

"I don't care," Yan interrupted. "I need you home in five minutes. We're supposed to leave, and I told the guys you were going to be there. They think you don't like them, and we need to nip that in the bud. These guys are important, and they can give me a real leg up. I need you here."

Daniel groaned. "I have a van full of dogs and snakes. I can't just drop them and leave." God, Yan thought the world revolved around him. And the reason his friends thought Daniel didn't like them was because he didn't. They were loud, brash, back-slapping ass-holes who played tricks on each other, as well as other people. It was childish shit that they should have grown out of a decade ago. "Go on and have fun with your friends. Tell them that something came up at work and that I'll be there as soon as I can." He needed to get out of this relationship sooner rather than later.

The line went dead—Yan's way of controlling the conversation. Daniel tried to stand up to him, but Yan always found a way to either cut Daniel off or steamroll over him. He needed to be stronger. But unlike Yan, Daniel hated veering into asshole territory. He placed his phone on the other seat, held the wheel tight in frustration, and continued the drive back to the shelter next to Mitchell and Beau's house.

"Do you need help?" Beau asked once he pulled in. "Where's Mitchell?"

"He's still there. He's probably getting ready to sedate the tiger about now." Daniel opened the back of the van.

"Tiger? You're kidding, right?" Beau asked, but Daniel shook his head. "What is he going to do with that? We don't have a place for it." Beau did not look happy.

"There's a large cage out back—I need to get that into the van. Mitchell thinks it should be big enough. Then we'll take down his current enclosure and reassemble it to house him here." Daniel shook his head. "The poor thing is probably sick and underfed. It's also endangered."

Beau gave him a small smile, then offered to settle the dogs in the quarantine area once Daniel got them unloaded. Then Daniel went back to the clinic, where he set up the tanks and heat lamps in the break room and fed and watered the snakes and tortoise. After he did a quick check of the other animals in the clinic, he hurried the mile or so back to the shelter, where he and Beau loaded the large animal cage into the van. And then Daniel finally headed back.

"I have the cage," Daniel said when he reached the house. "How is he?" He had so much energy, but he forced himself to stay calm around the tiger as he opened the back of the van.

Hank stood next to the cage with his hands on his hips. "Damn, he was hungry." The tiger's eyes were open, and he was alert, watching them. "Actually, he still looks hungry."

"He probably is. I only gave him a little bit at first. I needed to make sure he could keep it down before I fed him any more." Mitchell moved closer, and that large, regal head moved right along with him. Mitchell dropped some more meat inside, and the tiger chomped it down. "The tranquilizers in there should start to make him really sleepy in a little while. In the meantime, let's get the cage set up. As soon as he's out, we'll roll him in a blanket to move him and get him inside. Then we'll have to disassemble this enclosure and get on the road."

Daniel could feel Mitchell's tension mount as soon as the tiger was asleep. "How long will Raj be out?"

Mitchell smiled. "Raj?" Daniel nodded. "About two hours, maybe less. I didn't want to give him any more than what I did because I don't know what he weighs—we don't know how well he'll handle it."

With little time to spare, they got to work. Mitchell opened the door to the enclosure, and he and Daniel got Raj onto a blanket. Then, as soon as they had a straight shot, all three of them strained to lift the animal into the temporary cage. Once the door was closed, they slid it up the ramp and into the back of the van. Then they took the original cage apart and loaded the pieces into the van as well.

Daniel shook Hank's hand and said the usual things you said to people you hadn't seen in a while. Then they were on their way. Mitchell got on the phone and arranged for help to be waiting at the shelter near Mitchell's house when they arrived.

Once they got back, Mitchell and his friends re-built and reinforced the enclosure in record time. Then they moved Raj carefully inside. Mitchell took a blood sample and had just closed the door when Raj began to wake up.

"What are we going to do with him?" Beau asked.

Daniel gave him a lot of credit. Not everyone could deal with their husband bringing home stray animals... and a tiger.

"We need to find him a home, someplace he'll be properly cared for. I'll start making a few calls once I have him healthy. The poor thing was mistreated—just like all the others. But he's been well fed for now and has an appetite, which is good."

"You'd better come inside and get something to eat too," Beau said.

"I will. But first I have to check on the pups. They're going to need some attention as well," Mitchell said. "Give me half an hour or so." Then he took off for the barn that housed the shelter.

Daniel was tempted to follow. What he should do was get in his car and go to where Yan and his friends were. But he didn't want to do that. It was definitely time for him to tell Yan he needed to move out. It was over. It had been for a while. Helping Mitchell with the animals was his passion, and Yan was never going to understand that. Daniel deserved better.

And so did these animals. He turned to Raj and saw his eyes slide open.

"Hey, big guy," he said softly. "Lots of changes. But at least here, they should be for the better." Raj blinked at him, and Daniel could only hope that the changes *he* needed to make would go so smoothly.

Chapter 2

WESTON GREENWOOD STOOD outside the shelter, looking at the enclosure and wondering what a tiger was doing here. He'd been curious about it ever since he first saw the enclosure being built about two weeks ago. But he'd never dreamed he'd find a Sumatran tiger.

He wandered around the enclosure. It seemed that an area had been added to give the beautiful beast more room. Whoever had built it had also created a den of sorts on one end, allowing the cat to move away from prying eyes if he wanted to. The tiger watched him with a knowing gaze, his head moving slowly around to follow his motion.

"What are you doing here?" A man strode purposefully out of the barn. "Raj is dangerous. You could get hurt." His eyes blazed, and the tiger drew closer to the side of the enclosure as the man approached. The guy was cute—well, more than just cute—in an energetic way. He had blond hair that seemed to go in every direction all at once and big eyes as blue as the summer sky. *Handsome* wasn't the right word, Wes thought for a second as the jab of initial attraction welled and then settled in his belly. Maybe *delectable* was better.

"Is he bothering you?" the man said to the tiger in a soft voice, and the cat lifted itself up off the ground and moved to sit in front of him. Wes half expected the man to try to pet the beast, but he just stayed a step away from the fencing, the two of them watching each other. "What are you doing here?" he asked again, this time more gently. "You don't need to get close for Raj here to decide to hurt you."

The tiger opened his mouth in a yawn, displaying huge teeth before lying down again, still watching the other man. "I'm Weston—Wes. I came to ask for a job." Wes turned back to the tiger. "He's confused. And doesn't like being in a cage." Wes had always found animals easy to understand.

The man with the blond hair and pretty eyes scowled. He'd be stunning if not for the grumpy look. It didn't bother Wes, though. The guy was only protecting the tiger. That meant something to Wes.

"Well, we can't just let him run free, unfortunately. Not here. Can we, boy? But Mitchell is working on finding you a home where you'll have more space and maybe a lady tiger to spend your time with."

The back door of the house banged closed, and another man walked over to them. "Daniel?" he queried.

"Mitchell, this is Wes. I found him out here with Raj. He says he's looking for a job."

So the man's name was Daniel. He had nice eyes and a cute smile now that he wasn't scowling. Wes liked that.

"Mom said she saw an ad online that you were looking for some help with the dogs." Wes turned back to Raj, who loped into his den. He should probably explain further, but he'd always been a guy of few words. Most people talked too much, in his opinion. But he

needed to get this job, so he did his best to set his nat-
ural inclinations aside. "I'm really good with animals,
and they seem to like me. Sometimes I can tell how
they feel, in a way." He hoped that didn't sound dumb.

Mitchell nodded once. "I've been doing it myself,
along with help from Daniel here, for a year or so." He
turned toward the barn, and Wes figured Mitchell was
going to tell him to go home. "Come with me."

Wes followed Mitchell without saying anything
and went into the barn, where he saw a number of enclosures holding dogs. Most of them had a place inside
and then access to an outdoor run. The smaller dogs had
an indoor area where they could play. Several of the
dogs wagged their tails and bounded over, looking for
attention, their eyes bright. However, in the enclosure
at the far end lay a medium-sized dog, his eyes filled
with hurt.

"This is Reverend."

Looking closer, Wes gasped when he saw the scars
on the dog's reddish-brown coat. He went inside and
knelt down. Reverend didn't move except to turn his
head away, shaking a little. Wes could almost see the
pain this dog had experienced. His spirit had been injured—not just his body. Wes just sat, breathing deeply, letting calm wash over him, as he ignored Mitchell,
who stood outside. "It's okay," he said very softly, and
sure enough, Reverend turned his head. He had heard
him, so Wes spoke again, talking softly enough to just
tickle Reverend's ears. Wes ignored it when Daniel
joined Mitchell, though he felt the man's gaze on him,
heating the back of his neck. Wes swallowed, suppress-
ing the urge to turn to look at him, watching Reverend
instead.

No one said anything more, and then slowly Reverend got up with a sigh and came closer, curious, sniffing. Wes didn't move, but just allowed Reverend to take his time, doing whatever he needed to do. This poor dog had been really hurt, and he wore the scars of his tormentors on his skin and on his poor aching soul.

Wes understood that feeling far too well. He'd felt that same pain—had been hurt so badly by his father, someone he should have been able to trust. Maybe Reverend could sense it, because he came closer, and Wes held out his hand to let the dog smell his fingers. He made no move to close the distance between them, letting Reverend make the last move. When he did, Wes touched him with the tips of his fingers. He had always had an affinity with animals, an ability to understand them. Wes wished he could put it into words, but it was just part of him.

When Wes slowly stood and left the enclosure, Reverend hurried back to his corner. "Damn," Daniel said.

"We've been trying to get through to him for two weeks," Mitchell said. "Are you really interested in a shelter job?" He smiled happily, his expression open. Daniel did the same, the scowl from earlier now gone.

Wes nodded. He would much rather work around animals than people. He understood dogs and cats—what he didn't get was other people. Animals were simple creatures, and they didn't do things irrationally. They wanted food, water, and attention. They also lashed out when they thought they were in danger. That he could understand and live with.

It was people he just couldn't figure out. He'd spent a lot of his life dealing with a father whose erratic behavior he could never understand or trust. Wes had learned that it was best if he stayed quiet and made himself invisible.

"Excellent. We've finished the morning feeding already, but if you come back about five thirty, I'll take you through the evening routine. You should also bring your employment information so I can put you on payroll." Mitchell seemed pleased, and Wes smiled in return.

"Okay. I'll be here," Wes said and left the barn. Then he headed down the road toward home.

Once there, he went in the back door, being quiet so he didn't disturb his mother in case she was sleeping. He took off his shoes and walked softly through the small house back to his mother's bedroom. "How did it go?" she asked in a weak voice.

Wes hated that she kept getting more and more frail. He had always hoped that she would beat the cancer odds. But lately her eyes had lost some of their sparkle and her hair had become dull, her skin increasingly sallow. He'd given up his editing job in Philadelphia and moved back home six months ago to help care for her. The truth was that he hadn't liked the job, but it had been the only work he could find. He'd never figured out what he wanted to do long-term—he hadn't thought that far ahead—and right now, given his mom's health, it really didn't matter.

"I got the job," he answered, sitting in the chair next to her bed. He often sat there and talked to her. "Would you believe they've got a tiger there? He's beautiful, and his eyes are so intense...." He sighed.

"A tiger?" his mom asked, as if wanting to make sure she'd heard correctly.

"I get the impression Raj was mistreated. But he's doing well now, and they're trying to find a home for him in a zoo. But it's too bad he can't be taken home to the wild," he said softly.

His mom smiled and took his hand. "It's terrible that someone would abuse such a wild creature—any creature, really." A touch of anger colored her voice, and it was an emotion Wes shared. Wes should probably have been surprised that someone had even tried to keep a tiger as a pet, but he knew folks were capable of crueler things. "But he wouldn't survive in the wild," she said. "Yes, he's a wild animal, but he probably has no idea how to hunt. He was probably raised by people since he was a cub. No, sweetheart, it's best that he goes to a zoo, where he'll be well looked after." She coughed, and Wes gave her the glass of water he kept by the side of the bed, holding it while she sat up and drank.

"I suppose." He sat back as his mom grew quiet and then drifted off to sleep. Then he picked up the glasses on the bedside table and took them to the kitchen, rinsed everything out, and put them in the dishwasher. Finally he made a little lunch, simple food his mom could eat, and took a tray into the bedroom.

"You don't have to do this. I can drink some of that meal shake stuff," she said when Wes handed her a plate with a grilled cheese sandwich. She had a few bites, then sipped at the shake he'd put in the glass. As he ate his own sandwich, he sat back in the chair. His mom was a slow eater, which allowed him time to process the day's events.

He sighed as an image of Daniel flashed in his mind. The vet's assistant was kind of cute. Although Wes probably shouldn't be thinking about another man while sitting next to his mom. He had never talked to her about things like that. Though kids usually came out in their teens, at twenty-three, he hadn't told his mother he was gay. When he wasn't living at home, he had simply kept that part of his life to himself. Wes had intended to tell his mom, but then she got sick and it didn't seem so important. All that mattered was doing what he could to make sure she had the best chance of getting better.

Now it looked as if he'd never get the chance to tell her. After all, he wasn't sure how she'd react, and he couldn't take a chance that she'd get upset.

Wes had learned some time ago that it was best to keep his thoughts to himself. His father had taught him that the hard way. So, after taking away the dishes, he sat in front of the television to watch game-show contestants who couldn't seem to get any of the answers, wishing things were different.

Wes had always been quiet. In school, his teachers had encouraged him to participate, but he never had. And it wasn't that he didn't want to or that he was shy—he just wasn't the talkative type. He did talk, though, when he watched television. Wes couldn't understand why people had trouble completing the chain on the puzzle. The answers were obvious. His mother had often told him to try out for one of those shows, but he knew that would never happen. So he made guesses and answered questions along with the television, episode after episode, until it was time to go back to the shelter.

Once he had checked on his mother, he walked down the road to the shelter. No one was outside, so he knocked on the door.

"Are you Wes?" a rather handsome man asked, holding a toddler in his arms. "I'm Beau, and this is Jessica," he said. "Come on in a minute. Mitchell is still at the clinic. He had a last-minute intake." He pushed open the door.

Jessica squirmed, and Beau put her down. The little girl took off as soon as she was on her own feet, a small dog running right behind her. Wes smiled and followed Beau inside, then sat where he indicated.

"That's Randi. She was supposed to be Mitchell's dog, but she adopted Jessica, and that was the end of that." Jessica ran to the sofa and climbed up. Then the dog jumped up and settled in next to her.

"They know who they like," Wes said softly. Randi stood after a while, her tail going a mile a minute, and then she jumped down and bounded up onto Wes's lap. He gently petted her, and she soaked up the attention, then got down once Jessica started running around again.

"Would you like some coffee?" Beau asked.

Wes shook his head, then remembered his manners. "No, thank you." It was so much easier not to talk. Most people would simply forget he was there, and that way he wasn't in their line of fire.

Beau sat down. When Jessica ran by, he lifted the little girl up and tickled her. She giggled like crazy. Laughter was something Wes hadn't heard in a long time. With his mom in bed most of the time and him taking care of her, there wasn't anything particularly happy in the house. Still, he found himself smiling as he watched the two of them.

"How is your mom doing?" Beau asked. "Your neighbor's daughter and Jessica sometimes have play dates," he added as an explanation.

The question took Wes by surprise, the way it always did. Somehow, he didn't think others cared that much about them. "As well as possible, I guess," he answered.

"I used to see her at Dickinson all the time before she stopped working. Your mom is quite an amazing person," Beau said. "We worked together on the learning systems I design and build."

Wes nodded and smiled. His mom had been a professor at Dickinson College, where she had taught language studies. He used to go with her sometimes, sitting in the back of the class, listening in, when she hadn't been able to get a sitter. "Yes. She's very knowledgeable." His father had worked as a carpenter and had resented that his mother was so good at what she did.

"Your mom is more than knowledgeable. She's insightful and had the most wonderful ideas about the best way to teach people." Jessica settled on his lap, resting her head against his chest, and the dog lay next to the chair.

A car's tires crunched on the drive outside, and Wes craned to see out the window. When he saw Mitchell get out of his car, he excused himself and met Mitchell outside.

Mitchell brought him right out to the shelter, showed him where he kept the food and medicine, then explained the sheet that detailed what each dog was to get.

"What about Raj?" Wes asked.

"I'll take care of him. For now, I think it's best that I'm the only one who comes near him. Start on the dogs and let me know if you have any questions. Okay?"

Wes nodded and got to work. He carefully measured out food for each of the canines, then put their bowls inside their enclosures and made sure they ate. He also changed their water bowls and made sure to give some affection to all of them. The last dog for him to feed was Reverend. When Wes put his bowl in the enclosure, Reverend looked at him but didn't approach. Wes sat close to the bowl, staying still and calmly watching the dog. Wes could tell he was hungry, but the distrust in his eyes warred with the emptiness of his belly.

"It's okay," he said softly, just sitting there, being patient. And then Reverend got up and slowly walked over, head down, eyes up, as though he expected to be hit.

"Hey, Wes, I thought—" Daniel had come to the door of the shelter, but he stopped and stood still when he saw what Wes was doing. Wes was afraid Reverend would spook, but he came closer and took some food, and then backed away. He watched and ate before eyeing the bowl for more. He repeated the process, taking a mouthful of food and going off to eat before coming back. Once he was done, Reverend walked away back to the other side. Wes picked up the dish, left fresh water for him, and exited the enclosure.

"Wow," Daniel said, overflowing with excitement. "That was pretty amazing. He never eats until we all leave."

"Fear is a hard thing to get over… for a dog," Wes said, and thought he saw a bit of the same pain he'd seen in Reverend's eyes flash in Daniel's.

"Not just for dogs." Daniel gently bit his lower lip, making it red and a little puffy. Wes wanted to ask about what he'd said, but he figured it was Daniel's business. "Mitchell is out with Raj making sure he's eating too. I fed the snakes and tortoise at the clinic."

"You have those too?"

"We picked them up at the same place we found Raj and the six dogs back there. Mitchell is treating them, and with luck, he'll find homes for them soon." Daniel followed Wes to the door, still talking. "I just love all of them. That's why I'm hoping to become a veterinarian. Are you in college too?"

Wes shook his head. "I graduated a year ago." His mother's illness had changed any future plans he'd had.

"What did you study?" Daniel asked.

"Literature," he said. Then he turned away—it was better not to think about it. He looked over to see how Raj was faring. "Raj seems to like Mitchell." Man and beast stood motionless, watching each other, Raj's tail flicking every so often.

"How can you tell?" Daniel asked.

Wes wasn't sure how he knew—he just did. "I think it's the way his shoulders and back are relaxed. He isn't ready to pounce. He knows that Mitchell won't hurt him." He sighed and tried not to think about his own fears. Maybe his mother was right and he did need to get back out into the world. But that was the way of hurt, and Wes had already had enough of that in his life.

"Who's your favorite? Author, I mean?" Daniel turned to him with such earnestness, Wes had to smile. It was so rare for anyone to show that much interest in him that he forgot himself.

"That's like asking a parent to name their favorite child. I love so many writers. Ray Bradbury is an old love, and so is Isaac Asimov. I fell in love with science fiction at an early age and read all I could get my hands on. And Ursula Le Guin is a huge favorite of mine."

Daniel nodded. "*Left Hand of Darkness* was amazing," he said quietly, almost reverently. "I read a lot, but now I only have time for textbooks and veterinary science journals. I really want to be as good as Mitchell. He opened the practice here and then started the shelter, taking in dogs and other animals because he refused to put them down."

"I have to agree with him there." Sometimes Wes wondered if he should have studied veterinary medicine or become a zookeeper, which would allow him to work with animals all the time. He was sure he'd have loved that—he seemed to have some sort of connection with dogs, cats, and wild creatures. But literature was quiet and allowed him to spend time inside his head with his books. And if he was inside his head, he couldn't get hurt. Wes didn't need a psychologist to tell him that he'd made the decisions he'd made as a way to escape the way his father had treated him, wounding him physically and emotionally.

"How is everything?" Mitchell asked, walking back over toward them.

"Reverend came over and ate while Wes was sitting right next to him. It was amazing. Wes didn't touch him, but still, it was so awesome to see him responding to someone." Daniel grinned.

"You really seem to have a way with animals," Mitchell told him. Wes shrugged. He knew what it was—he understood pain. Still, Mitchell was happy, and that counted for something. "Come on inside for something to eat. We need to talk about tomorrow's schedule." He checked his watch as a truck pulled in the drive and came to a stop.

Two big men climbed out of the new-looking vehicle. They were well dressed and smiled as they pulled off their sunglasses, which they stashed on the dashboard before approaching.

"Can I help you?" Mitchell said.

"I understand you have dogs for adoption," one of the men said. "My friend and I have been looking for a pet, and we thought we'd give a couple of deserving dogs a home."

"Right now, we have fifteen dogs in the shelter ready to be adopted, with some more that were recently rescued and in quarantine." Mitchell seemed happy and led the men toward the shelter. The dogs all perked up, tails wagging, some prancing as though they knew they needed to put on a show to get noticed. They hurried close as Mitchell made introductions.

Wes watched them as Mitchell spoke, noticing how the men looked the dogs over but rarely touched any of them, and if they did, it was to offer a light pat on the head. That didn't sit right with Wes. People looking to adopt a dog got down to their level and got to know them. They interacted with them. If Wes was in this situation, he'd have been on the floor playing with the dogs, getting a feel for his new pet.

He held back and motioned to Daniel. "Do not let these men adopt any dogs," he said very quietly as alarm bells went off in the back of his head. "Something about this isn't right." Somehow he just knew, but it was hard for him to explain. So what if they weren't petting the dogs enough? It felt like a flimsy excuse. He closed his mouth, wishing he could explain better.

"What about that one?" the second man asked, pointing to Reverend. Up until then, he'd been quiet. "He looks like a good dog for me."

Wes practically bit his lower lip hard enough to draw blood. There was no way Reverend was a good fit for anyone right now, and judging by the way Reverend tried to hide, he knew it too.

The man opened the door, went into Reverend's enclosure, and walked right up to the crouching dog. "Please be—" Mitchell called as the man reached out to stroke one of Reverend's ears, and the dog snapped hard. The man pulled his hand away, grasping his fingers.

"That's enough," Wes growled, something inside him not able to take any more. "You all need to go now. Right now!" He raised his voice and pointed toward the door. "You aren't good enough to adopt any of these dogs. I suggest you leave."

"Hey," the first man said, puffing himself up. He turned to Mitchell. "I thought you wanted to find homes for these dogs."

"Good homes, not any home." He closed the door to Reverend's enclosure once the man ran out. "I suggest you leave now. I don't think any of my animals will be a good fit for you." He glared, and the men turned toward the door and left the barn, both looking back inside.

"You're making a mistake," the second man said.

"I don't think so. Dogs have good instincts," Mitchell said, following them out.

Then all three of them waited until they turned their truck around and left.

Wes went back into the barn, grabbed a pen and a scrap of paper, and jotted down the tag number from the truck.

"Do you want to explain what happened?" Mitchell asked. "I didn't like them either, but…." He didn't seem to be questioning Daniel's judgment as much as confirming his own intuition.

Wes shook his head. "They weren't looking to adopt. They wanted dogs for something else—not as pets." He knew that as surely as he knew his name. "What kind of man walks up to a dog that's scared to death and reaches for it? Did you see him? He'd already pulled his hand back before Reverend reacted. He *expected* him to snap at him. Maybe that was what he wanted—a dog that would fight back."

Mitchell didn't move. He was looking down the drive where the men had gone. "Bastards," he said under his breath.

"What do we do if we see them again?" Daniel asked between clenched teeth.

"Call the police. But I doubt they'll be back. If they want fighting dogs, they'll get them somewhere else," Mitchell said.

Wes's gaze moved from Mitchell to Daniel. He could tell that both men were as angry as Wes was. He hoped Mitchell was right, but he wasn't going to count on it. He knew men like them, and they seldom took no for an answer.

Chapter 3

ONCE THE shelter was closed up for the night, Daniel said good night to Mitchell.

"Did you walk over?" he asked Wes. "Would you like a ride home?" He found himself smiling for no apparent reason. He shouldn't be this turned around when he was near Wes, not when he was technically still with Yan, but the man just made his pulse race whenever they were together. He had expressive eyes and broad shoulders. He might even have played football, though he didn't seem the type. Hell, the guy could have been intimidating if he hadn't been so quiet, even kind of shy, in a way that only drew Daniel's interest even more.

Wes hesitated but then nodded. "Thanks." The sky had clouded over, with the clouds darkening and getting lower to the ground.

"No problem," Daniel said.

"Can I check on Raj first?" Wes asked, but he was already heading over. The tiger was inside his den, but as Wes spoke to him, he loped out and came over to sit in front of him. Wes knelt a couple feet from the metal, just looking back. "I know. You're confused and maybe a little scared. But these are good people, and they'll find you a forever home, just like they do with the dogs."

Raj opened his mouth and chuffed softly, as if he knew what Wes was saying. Daniel just stood there, mesmerized by the way Wes seemed to connect with the big cat.

"You look a lot better than you did a few days ago, big guy. That's good to see." Raj had lost some of his emaciated appearance and was starting to fill out a little, thank goodness. Mitchell thought that the tiger probably had worms and maybe even an infection. Luckily, whatever his problems had been, the medicine they'd been slipping in his food was taking care of it.

"He really is beautiful," Daniel said, standing next to Wes. "I thought so when I first saw him."

Wes nodded. "It must have been pretty awful for him."

Daniel nodded slowly, turning to Wes. "He was underweight—Mitchell thought he'd been underfed for a while. We're probably lucky he didn't attack us right away out of sheer hunger. We got him here and Mitchell started feeding him more, though it costs a lot every day."

"Is he any closer to finding a place for him?" Wes asked.

Daniel swallowed. He hated the thought of the big cat leaving, but he knew Mitchell couldn't house him permanently, even if he could get the permits required. The food alone cost a fortune. "I don't know. Mitchell is determined to get him healthy first, but I think he's been in touch with a few locations. There are a couple of zoos with tiger breeding programs. Since he's endangered, that would be the best-case scenario, but none of them can take him right away." The truth was that Daniel liked having Raj here. Daniel wasn't scared of the tiger, but he respected his power.

"I know that's best for him, but I kind of like being this close to him and getting to know him." Wes didn't look away until eventually Raj strode back into his den.

When Wes turned to leave, Daniel said, "Let me drop you off at home."

Wes nodded and they headed for the car. Daniel followed Wes's easy directions and pulled into the drive of a small but well-kept house. He waited for Wes to get out.

"Thank you," Wes said softly, but he didn't get out of the car. Daniel watched and found Wes eyeing him up as if he was trying to puzzle something out. "What's wrong?" Wes seemed confused; then his eyes grew soft and his expression filled with empathy.

There was no need to lie—not that he could, given the knowing way Wes was looking at him. "My boyfriend," Daniel said. "I don't want to go home because I need to tell him to get out of the apartment. But Yan just steamrolls over me or changes the subject whenever I say something he doesn't like." He sighed, gripping the steering wheel as though it were a lifeline. "He can get manipulative," he added softly, wishing he'd kept quiet.

Wes narrowed his eyes. "Does he hurt you?"

Daniel was an instant from denying it… then hung his head instead. He felt like such a coward. But every time he got up the nerve to say something, Yan either changed the subject or just talked over him until Daniel gave up. And if he didn't, Yan gave him something else to think about.

"It's not your fault," Wes said, his jaw set in the same way it had been when he'd yelled at those men to leave the shelter.

Daniel wondered why he was still sitting there. This was his problem, not Wes's. Heck, he barely knew

him, and he'd basically just admitted to Wes that he was
a coward. "This is my mess, and I have to figure it out."

Wes shrugged but still didn't get out of the car.

"I should do that now."

Wes continued sitting there. "Then let's go."

Daniel tried to process what Wes was saying. "You
want to come with me?" The idea did have merit. Yan
wouldn't to be able to push him around as easily if he
had backup. So before Wes could change his mind,
Daniel turned around and headed into town.

Daniel's apartment was five minutes away, on the
north side of Carlisle, in a four-unit building out in the
alphabet streets. He parked in one of the visitor spots
because Yan had put his huge-ass truck in the parking
space dedicated for their unit, the way he always did.
Daniel turned off the engine and sat still, not wanting
to get out.

"You will never be free of him until you stand your
ground," Wes said gently. Then he got out of the car and
waited for Daniel to follow suit.

Daniel knew he needed to get this over with. But he
was tired and could have used some time to rest. Still, he
knew Wes was right. It was time.

He led the way up into the building, walking a little
taller knowing Wes had his back. In fact, he felt a hell
of a lot more like his old self—something he hadn't experienced in a while. With his usual energy returning,
he bounded up the stairs to his place, unlocked the door,
and walked inside.

Yan was definitely home—his truck was parked
outside—but the apartment was quiet. Daniel checked
the kitchen and then opened the bedroom door. He
found Yan kneeling on the bed, another guy's legs on
either side of him.

Daniel couldn't believe what he was seeing. Still, he managed to ask, "How long has this been going on?"

Yan paused midthrust. "You don't give me what I want, so what do you care if I get it elsewhere?" Then, without another word, he went back to fucking the guy... who barely looked legal.

Daniel was speechless and mortified... and yet, in an odd way, relieved. Yan had gone too far this time.

"Get *out*!" Wes snapped harshly.

The kid slipped off the bed, gasping before finding his colt-like legs. He grabbed clothes to hold in front of him and then dashed toward the bathroom. Daniel let him go.

"What the fuck do you think you're doing?" Yan surged forward, his arm raised... until Wes grabbed it.

"That's enough. You're leaving too," Wes said, his voice deep and deadly. He tugged Yan off the bed. "Put some damned clothes on your bony ass and get out of here."

"Yes," Daniel said, finding his voice again. "This is my place—my name is on the lease. Go live with that kid if you want. But you're not staying here anymore." He opened the closet door and began throwing Yan's clothes on the floor. Once the last hanger was down, he hit his drawers and added more of his stuff to the pile. "I'd start packing if I were you. Anything you leave behind will be tossed out the window." Damn, he felt good, empowered in a way he hadn't been in a long time.

"Leave my shit alone," Yan snapped, then yelped. The sound of a sharp smack filled the room. "What the fuck was that for?" He whirled on Wes, rubbing his backside.

"Just getting the attention of the jackass in the room. Get dressed, get your shit, and get out." Wes crossed his arms over his wide chest, standing like a silent sentinel near the door. Daniel felt his resolve increasing by the second.

"I want you gone. You're a jerk, and I'm better off without you." He tried his best to look Yan in the eye, but the guy was naked and he had always been amazing to look at. "So just get out."

"Is that what you really want?" Yan asked, using that hurt puppy tone that always made Daniel back down. He hated it. But this time it had the opposite effect on Daniel—he now saw it for what it was. He had been used and controlled for months, always letting Yan have his way. As much as Daniel had thought he'd loved him, the idea of spending any more time with Yan sent a chill up his spine.

"Yes. Take your stuff and go."

"Where?" Yan asked, using that damned tone again.

"That's not my problem," Daniel said with more force. "Now get dressed and get out." He was done with this shit.

"You little—" Yan raised his hand once more, and once again, Wes grabbed it. This time he pushed Yan back against the door with a thud.

Yan's eyes widened as he finally seemed to get the message. He pulled on some pants and began gathering his clothes in his arms, then hurried out the door. Daniel grabbed some of them as well, then walked across the room, opened the front window, and shoved them out, smiling as the fabric fluttered down to the lawn.

"Just thought I'd help," Daniel called. He retrieved more articles of clothing and threw them out as well, covering the shrubbery out front with socks and under-wear. God, he felt lighter. And while he might not be exactly happy, the cloud that had been shadowing his life seemed to be lifting. He grabbed one last pile of shirts and tossed them out the window, but he didn't stay to watch them hit the ground.

"Is there anything else of his left?" Wes asked, looking out the window, where Yan yelled and swore. Daniel peeked over Wes's shoulder as Yan snatched up his purple jockey shorts from the rose bushes.

"Not much. Just a few more things." Daniel picked up the last few items and went over to the window. "Catch." He tossed out Yan's phone and iPad. Yan caught them and forgot to hold up his pants. He flashed half the neighborhood before he could yank them up again. "He always did have a great ass. Too bad that turned out to be his very best quality." He found Yan's keys and, after he took the apartment ones off, sent the rest of them sailing out as well. Finally, Daniel closed the window and watched as Yan loaded the rest of his stuff into his truck and sped away, probably still swearing up a storm. But at this point Daniel didn't care. He was rid of him, and that felt damned good—like his spirit could relax for the first time in months. "Thank you."

"You did it all. I was only here for support," Wes told him.

Daniel took a deep breath and smiled, then motioned to the sofa he'd bought at a secondhand store in town. Wes sat down while Daniel went into the kitchen and put together some snacks. He wasn't sure what Wes would want, so he brought everything he had. Wes took a Coke and popped open the can, then sipped from it before munching on a few chips. "What are you planning to do with your degree?" Daniel asked, trying to think of something to talk about.

Wes shrugged. "I haven't decided yet." He took another sip, then looked around the apartment and settled back, seemingly content to just sit. But Daniel wasn't all that comfortable with silence. He searched around for something to talk about, but he wasn't sure Wes was interested in conversing. He seemed more likely to talk Raj, or maybe Reverend.

"I graduated from Dickinson in May, and I'm trying to get into a really good veterinary program. My parents helped me as much as they could, but it's expensive. My dad is a school teacher in Michigan, outside Lansing, and Mom works part-time as a server in a restaurant, so they have enough to do just making ends meet." Daniel had managed to get his undergraduate degree on his own. Now he'd just have to find the money to take the next step. "I've applied at a few schools, and I'm waiting to hear back. I can't really afford to go this fall, so I thought I'd take a year to work and get some money together, then start next year. I'll have to move regardless of where I go—there aren't any schools with veterinary programs anywhere around here." He sipped a can of root beer, waiting for Wes to say something, but he just sat still, listening, so Daniel prattled on. "I've never had a pet, and now I realize how much I missed. Dad said he was allergic, but since he now has a dog, I know that was a lie. He just couldn't be bothered. And Mom went along with him—at least until she kicked him to the curb."

Wes paled, then set his soda on the coffee table. He didn't say anything, but for a second it looked like he wanted to. Daniel waited, looking into his eyes, almost willing him to open up. Wes's beautiful deep brown eyes filled with a hurt that Daniel understood, and he wondered just how close their experiences were. But he also knew that pressing Wes wasn't going to get him any answers.

He reached for a few chips at the same time Wes did, and their hands brushed against each other. A heated zing flashed through him. Wes just watched him and then slowly pulled his hand away. Daniel could almost feel his gaze. Wes seemed to have such hidden depths, and that intrigued Daniel, making him wonder what was under that unflappable exterior of his. But it also worried him a little, because he didn't know if the attraction was mutual. Maybe if the guys he liked were more open, he wouldn't fall for assholes like Yan.

As Daniel finished up his soda, Wes got up and looked out the window. Daniel realized it was time for him to go home. "Thank you for being here. I've needed to get him out of the apartment and my life for a few weeks now, but…." His cheeks heated with embarrassment.

"I saw how he reacted. I know what it feels like to live in fear," Wes said. "No one should be afraid in their own home." He smiled slightly, and Daniel felt some of the roiling inside him—something he'd been experiencing for weeks—finally begin to settle, like a twisting drain running out of water. "I should go."

Daniel nodded, took care of the snacks and empty soda cans, then led Wes out to his car. He checked it over in case Yan had decided to damage it. Then he drove back out of town to Wes's house. "Thank you again."

"Hopefully he's gone for good and you can move on now." Then, without another word, Wes got out of the car and headed up the walk and into the house. Daniel didn't back away until Wes was inside.

Daniel hoped that Wes was right and that Yan was truly gone, but he wasn't holding his breath. Yan could be a persistent asshole. Still, with Wes's backup, Daniel had been able to give Yan the boot. That was the first step. Now he just had to put the rest of his life back together. In some ways, that was going to be even harder.

Chapter 4

"YOU DON'T need to sit here for hours just keeping me company," Wes's mom said when he found her out of bed, sitting in the living room, two mornings later.

"I need to get to work at the shelter," he said. "But I can get you something to eat before I leave." He headed for the kitchen.

"I already had a shake and some toast. I couldn't sleep, so I got up earlier." She actually smiled, and for the first time in weeks, Wes could see some color in her cheeks. But he tried not to get too excited. They had seen progress before, only for his mom to decline once again. "Go on to work, and I'll stay here and watch television for a while." She waved him away, and Wes left the house, feeling a little lighter as he walked toward the shelter in the early morning sunshine.

The rain they'd had the night before had freshened everything up. The fields sparkled with water droplets that caught the sun. The air smelled clean—like it was new and he was the first person to breathe it in. Once Wes reached the shelter, he walked past the entrance and went to Raj's enclosure, where the tiger sat watching him. The big cat yawned as though he too were just waking up, and Wes caught it from him, yawning in response. "Did you like the rain?" Wes asked. Raj blinked at him and then stretched his long legs upward against the bars, claws lengthening as his paws stretched. Then he settled back down and returned to his den. "I know just how you feel. All this strength, and yet you can't seem to do anything with it." Wes was strong and he could do just about anything, but he couldn't give any of it to his mother to help her fight the cancer. That she had to do on her own. And Wes had never felt more helpless in his life.

Turning away from the enclosure, he entered the shelter and began making up food bowls. Excitement ramped up as he fed each pup and then let them in their runs to burn off some of their energy.

"Are you going to be more sociable today?" Wes asked Reverend as he set down the bowl, then sat down in the dog's enclosure the way he had all the previous days. "You know I'm not going to hurt you." He kept talking quietly, and Reverend approached the bowl, almost on his belly. Wes hated to see him so scared. This time he nibbled at the food in the bowl, and as he did, Wes gently encouraged him. "You're a good dog," Wes whispered. "Yes, you are."

Reverend ate quickly, and once the bowl was empty, he looked at Wes as if wondering about getting closer. Wes held still, and this time when Reverend backed away, Wes sighed with a slight smile and left the enclosure.

"I can't decide if you talk more to him or to the tiger," Daniel said. "You don't talk much to the rest of us." He tilted his head to the side. "Are you one of those strong, silent types?"

Wes shrugged. "I just don't feel like always filling the air with chatter, I guess." He closed up the food and made sure the bin lids were on tight so no mice would get in.

"Oh, I guess I talk too much sometimes and…." Daniel trailed off.

Wes blinked. "I wasn't talking about you." He hadn't been thinking of Daniel at all when he'd said that. "My father used to talk all the time. He'd impart his wisdom—as though it was being handed down from God himself—often at the top of his voice. I couldn't argue with him because I was just a kid, so I quickly learned not to even try." He finished making sure all the supplies were properly stowed, and then he closed the supply room door. "The few times I tried to stand up to him, I was rewarded with a slap on the face… or worse. If I was lucky, he'd just ignore me. Mom would stand up for me when my father got physical, but otherwise…." He shrugged. Wes just figured his dad was the way he was, and that was it. For Wes, it was water under the bridge. "He wasn't a particularly nice person, and he had a real temper, especially when he'd been drinking."

Wow, that was a lot for Wes to say at one time, and it surprised him. Daniel realized that his own situation must have touched Wes as well. "You felt helpless," Daniel said. "Like I did with Yan." He drew closer. "Except thanks to you, I was able to escape. You were just a kid, and you were stuck there." Daniel seemed to understand, and Wes found himself nodding. "That must have been terrifying at times."

"He was my dad, and I didn't know any better until later. But I grew up. The last time he hit me, I hit him back, only harder. At that point I wasn't a little kid anymore, and I had come to dislike my own father."

He took a deep breath and released it slowly, growing quiet for a few seconds. Daniel wondered if Wes had said all he wanted to, but then he surprised Daniel once again and continued. "I didn't speak to him after that, and a month later, Mom left him, for more reasons than just his increasingly erratic behavior. And I haven't seen him since. He's an abusive out-of-control alcoholic who never met a vice he didn't like. When I was younger, he once took me to an underground gambling den, and I heard him talking on the phone, making bets on some unsavory event. He was a real piece of work, let me tell you." He had learned a great deal about that world from his father, even if his dad hadn't known about it at the time. He hadn't talked about his father in years, and he wasn't sure exactly why he was opening up to Daniel, other than he had a feeling the younger man would understand.

"And your mom is ill, right? I think that's what Mitchell said. Is she getting better?" Daniel asked.

Wes shrugged. "I'd like to think that she will." It was the best answer he had. His mother had been fighting for long enough that they deserved some sort of good news. She hadn't had any energy in a while, so he was taking the fact that she got up this morning as a good sign. Wes didn't even want to think that it could be some kind of "last good day" sort of thing. "Do you need to go to the office?"

"Yeah, but I wanted to check on the dogs that we have in isolation. They are all looking better, and Mitchell says they can be made available for adoption in a few days." He checked the time and hurried toward the door. "A man is coming in to look over the snakes. Apparently he's interested in adopting both of them, and Mitchell is ready for them to go to good homes. We usually just work with dogs, but Mitchell wasn't about to turn away an animal in need." From the attractively fierce look in Daniel's eyes, he felt the same.

"What about their former owner?" Wes asked.

Daniel paused. "His fall was apparently pretty bad. His family had to place him in a long-term care home. He was really broken up but is relieved that his pets will be well cared for and has given Mitchell permission to find them new homes." Daniel waved, then hurried out of the shelter.

Wes finished up feeding all the dogs, then took some time to play with each of them. They all wanted attention so badly, and he scratched ears and rubbed heads and bellies. It never ceased to amaze him how people could not want one of these guys. His last stop was at Reverend, and he watched the dog as he lay on a blanket in the corner. Wes went inside and knelt down just to see what the dog would do. There was such longing and hurt in those huge brown eyes. He waited and spoke softly until Reverend stood and slowly walked over to him. The need in those eyes was so deep, it touched Wes's soul. He knew what it felt like to be so hurt and confused that he didn't know which way to turn or who to trust. All Reverend needed was a chance and a little patience.

"I'm not going to hurt you," Wes promised as Reverend drew closer. Finally, Reverend got close enough that Wes could lightly stroke his head. "You're a good boy." He scratched his ears and stroked his back, giving the animal as much love and attention as he dared. "Yes, you are. Someone really hurt you, but I'll never do that." He continued petting the dog, and Reverend leaned against him, so starved for attention and yet afraid to ask for it. "I know what it feels like to be all bottled up." He smiled as Reverend's gaze met his. "Maybe it's time for both of us to let someone else in."

WES SPENT the afternoon with his mom, who'd sat up the entire time. She returned to bed just before he left to do the evening feeding at the shelter. He made sure she had something to drink, then left the house, feeling happy. Mom actually had some energy for the first time in months. His steps were lighter as he strode up the road and turned into the shelter drive.

"I already told you both to leave." Mitchell's voice carried from inside as Wes passed the black truck that had been at the shelter the other day. His heartbeat sped up, and he pulled out his phone and called the police as he hurried inside.

"What's going on?" Wes asked, seeing two huge men standing over Mitchell—two different men. "I already called the police, and they're on the way." He put his phone in his pocket.

The men looked at each other and then moved toward the door. Wes stood aside as they left the barn and went back to their truck.

"What's with them?" Wes asked Mitchell.

"They showed up ten minutes ago, just as two other families were leaving. One of the families adopted Petey, the little beagle mix. Anyway, those two were looking over each of the dogs, and I don't know why, but they just set my teeth on edge." He stood straighter. "I couldn't let them take any of the dogs—it didn't feel right."

Wes had had that same feeling. "When the police arrive, you might want to give them the license plate I copied down last time." He found the paper where he'd written it down. "Just in case. Though they really haven't done anything wrong. At least not yet." He took a deep breath. "They were interested in Reverend, Boxer, and Forrest, right?" They were all large, strong dogs. Reverend was part boxer, and the other two were German shepherd mixes. All three of them were gentle, but an idea had tickled the back of his mind since the last time that truck was here.

Wes really didn't want to think about what they wanted the dogs for. "Reverend tried to bite the last guy who was here. He hated him on sight, which told me something wasn't right. Maybe these guys are looking for fighters, or bait animals." He went right over to Boxer, scratched the dog's ears, then did the same with Forrest, and finally went to Reverend, who approached slowly but allowed him to give him some affection as well. "They're all good dogs, and that…." He shivered. "That sort of thing is terrible." He continued stroking Reverend gently before leaving him alone to start getting food together.

Once the police arrived, they looked things over and spoke to Mitchell while Wes finished working, bringing in the dogs from their runs and making sure they were bedded down for the night. Once they were all set, Wes got a leash and approached Reverend. He clipped the leash onto his collar. Then he took him out into the evening air to let him explore.

Reverend was definitely a sniffer, checking out all the interesting smells in the area, including the wheels of the police car. The officer finished speaking to Mitchell and then left while Wes took Reverend around to the front yard, away from all the excitement and Raj. He didn't know how the dog would react to the tiger, and he didn't really want to find out. Still, Reverend seemed to enjoy the walk, even if he constantly watched Wes before they headed back toward the shelter.

"What did they say?" Wes asked.

"They're going to look into it. Apparently there have been reports of a dogfighting ring farther out in the country. The officer said that we were right to be careful and that getting the license plate number was smart."

"I should put Reverend back inside." He gently scratched the animal's head.

"You know, you've done wonderful work with him. I figured it was going to take months to bring him out of his shell, and you've accomplished it in less than a week."

"He'll always be skittish, but he just needed to trust that he wasn't going to be hurt."

Wes headed inside, wondering where Daniel was. He'd been coming around after work the past few days, and Wes missed seeing him. He wanted to ask Mitchell about it, but if Daniel wanted to go home, that wasn't any of Wes's business. Still, Wes wished he'd been around. If he was honest with himself, he looked forward to seeing Daniel.

Daniel always seemed to have so much energy, and he'd talk about anything. Wes had never realized how quiet his world had become until Daniel became part of it. Now Wes missed his chatter as he gave each dog a treat and closed up the supply cupboard. He hoped Daniel was okay and that Yan hadn't decided to come back and make Daniel miserable.

Mitchell met him on his way out. "Beau and I are going to be gone the weekend after next. Do you think you'll be able to take care of things here? I'll have some meat cut up for Raj that you'll just need to drop into his cage. Don't even try to open the door. I'll hose out the outside area when I get back on Sunday."

"Of course." Wes brushed off his hands and peeked into Reverend's enclosure. The dog looked at him forlornly, as if he had discovered something special and now it was gone.

"Have you ever given any thought to a dog?" Mitchell asked. "Does your mom like animals?"

Wes chuckled. "Mom loves them, but with her being sick, I haven't really thought about getting a pet." She was alone a lot of the time, though, and he worried about her.

"I don't usually do this, but if you want to take Reverend home with you and see how he reacts to your mom, you can do that any time."

"Mitchell... I...."

"One of the things you learn when you run a shelter is that we can't let every dog bond with us. But I think Reverend has already done that with you. He trusts you, and that isn't an easy thing for a pup like him to do."

"I know. But I'm not sure if it's a good idea. What if he and my mom don't get along?" Wes turned to watch Reverend settle down in the very corner, as if he was trying to hide once again. Sometimes he swore that dog knew what they were saying.

"But what if they do?" Mitchell asked.

Wes was tempted as he continued to watch the dog. Reverend got up and slowly crept over to him, as if he was promising he'd be good and not get into trouble. Wes knew it was all him projecting his emotions and confusion on the dog, but he found himself grabbing one of the leashes, opening the door, and connecting the leash to Reverend's collar.

"Take some food with you so you have some and a couple of the dishes out of the supply room. You can bring them back if it doesn't work out." Mitchell's suppressed smirk said that he already knew those things were never coming back. "I'll see you tomorrow morning." Mitchell strode back toward the house, and Wes closed up the kennel doors, then took Reverend's leash and walked back to his place.

More than once, he paused when a car came down their side of the road so he could make sure Reverend was well out of harm's way. As he waited, he wondered again if Daniel was okay. He wished he had Daniel's number just so he could message him or something. Maybe he was worrying over nothing. He hoped so.

"WES," HIS mom called when he came into the house.

"It's me. Are you in bed?" He led Reverend through the house and into the bedroom, where his mom sat up watching television.

"What did you bring me?" she asked, spying Reverend. His mom patted the bed, and Reverend jumped right up onto it and settled next to her as if he belonged there. "He's beautiful," she said, petting the dog's head. "What happened to him?"

"He was hurt pretty bad. Mitchell sewed him up, but he's very shy. I worked with him, and I think he's bonded with me." He sat on the side of the bed, and Reverend scooted over to lie right next to his side, his head on Wes's leg.

"I'd say so. He's a real pretty color."

Wes turned to her. "Is it okay if he stays here?"

His mom smiled. "Honey, if you were joining a twelve-man band, I'd let them all stay here." She patted his hand. "Your father hurt you badly, I know that. He hurt us both, in a lot of ways. Part of that is my fault for not seeing what he was doing to you at first, and then, when I did, not doing something about it sooner. I was trying to figure my own way out, and it was like swimming upstream against a fast current. I'm sorry I didn't act sooner. I really am." She sounded tired. "And after I got sick, you closed yourself off to everything and everyone. You can't keep doing that. So if this beautiful boy is the first creature you've decided to open up to, I'm going to welcome him. And when you're out working, he can keep me company." She stroked his back, and Reverend turned to look at her.

"I think he startles easily," Wes said.

"Then we'll need to be careful," his mom said, still smiling.

When Wes went to the kitchen, Reverend jumped down and followed him through the house. "Are you hungry? You know you ate already," Wes said as the dog sat next to his feet, wagging his stubby tail, big eyes looking up. Wes made a quick dinner of soup and a turkey sandwich. He gave Reverend a few pieces of chicken in his bowl as a treat and took his mom's dinner in to her, placing the tray over her lap.

"How is your friend? The one you helped the other day?" She took a sip of broth and a few bites. It was so good to see her eating again. As he settled in the chair, he realized she hadn't been sick in days. That was another improvement.

"I don't know. I didn't see him around today." He rested back in the chair to eat his own sandwich, with Reverend pressed against his legs. "I know I don't have any reason to be, but I'm worried."

"Why?" His mom leaned back against the padded headboard. She closed her eyes, and Wes grew quiet. "I'm not shuffling off this mortal coil, just resting a minute. What's got you all wound up?"

Wes set his plate on the side table. "Dad," he answered. "I thought we got rid of him, but he kept coming back." Each time drunk and determined to use his fists. "We kicked Daniel's cheating bastard boyfriend out of his place, but what if he comes back?"

"Then call him."

"I don't have his number."

She sighed. "You know where he lives. So get in my car and drive over there. Go see him if you're so worried. It's okay to care about your friends and to want to make sure they're okay. That's what people do."

He was such a non-people person most of the time, he was never quite sure how to act. He didn't have much patience for drama, and in the back of his mind, he knew he was worried people would treat him the way his father had. As a result, he often felt like he was on the outside looking in. But dogs and even tigers? They didn't judge or think he was weird just because he was quiet, the way many people seemed to.

Reverend sat up, his front paws on Wes's knees. Wes patted his legs, and Reverend jumped into his lap, making Wes exhale loudly. A sixty-pound lapdog. Well, he wasn't going to complain as Reverend settled across his legs, his head against Wes's chest. "Will you be okay?"

"I'm fine," his mom said. "Go check on your friend, and Reverend and I will get to know each other."

Wes lifted Reverend and placed him on the bed next to his mom. The dog watched his every move, then jumped down and followed him through the house and to the back door. He looked forlornly through the glass as Wes went to the car. He was tempted to just let him come, but Wes wasn't sure how well he'd do in the car… or what situation he'd be walking into.

Wes wondered if he was crazy as he headed toward Carlisle. But still, he drove to Daniel's building. He parked out front and looked up at the window Daniel had tossed Yan's clothes through, guessing the white bit of cloth on the ground under one of the shrubs was one of Yan's T-shirts. Wes got out, headed up the walk, and rang the bell for Daniel's place. He shifted his weight from foot to foot, listening as someone came down the stairs.

Daniel peered out the cracked-open door and then it opened more fully. Wes stifled a gasp at the puffiness around Daniel's dull eyes. It was as if his life source had been sucked away. "What happened?" he asked as Daniel stepped back. Wes came inside and followed him up to the apartment. Once they were inside, Daniel seemed to grow smaller. "Was it Yan?" Wes asked.

Daniel nodded, standing a little taller after a few steadying breaths.

"He was here when I got back from work yesterday. He said he was getting the rest of his things, but I didn't know he had another key." Wes went forward and hugged Daniel to him, hoping it was the right thing to do. "He was trying to take things that were mine, and I wouldn't let him."

Wes saw that the television that had been there was gone. "If he stole from you, then we need to call the police."

Daniel noticed the direction of his glance. "The TV was his, though I should have chucked it out the window too." Finally a bit of his usual feistiness came through in his voice. "I told him to leave, but he started whining, wanting to come back. When that didn't work, he screamed and raised his fists." Daniel's speech broke for a few seconds, and Wes held him tighter. Daniel took a deep breath. "This time I didn't take it. I yelled back at him, then grabbed the key from his front pocket. He actually let me do it—he thought I was getting frisky, the dope. Then I pushed him until I got him out the door."

Wes stood still, just holding him. Daniel felt good in his arms, close and warm. Wes could feel a touch of excitement starting to build inside him. Daniel might be smaller than him, but his fierceness—with the dogs and in standing up to Yan—lit a fire inside Wes.

"You got him to go?" Wes asked, and Daniel nodded, still clinging to him.

"Once he was outside, I locked the door, and he eventually left." Daniel seemed to steady himself, and Wes closed his eyes, breathing in his scent that was fresher now that the panic seemed to have passed.

"Then you did it," Wes said quietly. "You pushed him out. I know you got a little bruised, but you gave as good as you got. Right?" Wes asked.

Daniel stepped back, his eyes wide, and then he smiled and put his hand over his face before pointing to a spot on the carpet. "Better, I think. That's his blood. I think I might have broken his nose and split his lip. I'm not really sure. Once I started hitting him, I didn't stop until I slammed the door closed." He smiled once more and finally laughed nervously, the sound close enough to tears that Wes wasn't sure what it was meant to be. "But what do I do if he comes back?"

Wes hesitated and then made a decision. "Pack a bag. Mom and I have a small guest room at the house.

You can stay there for a few days if you like." At least he'd know that Daniel was okay. "Or maybe you could stay with some friends until you can get the landlord to change the locks."

"But what if he comes back and decides to break in? I got the key he had, but he could have made others...." He took a deep breath.

"At least you won't be here. And it's probably a good idea to bring anything valuable with you. At least it will give you a chance to think things over with other people around. If he does come back, you can call the police and let them handle it. And in the meantime, contact the landlord and get that lock changed. He might be able to get to it faster than you think."

Wes could see Daniel sitting in the apartment, scared and alone, wondering for hours if Yan was going to come back. Wes had been through that after his mother had kicked his father out of the house. After that, he'd come at both of them. Wes hadn't slept well for a long time afterward, jumping at any sound he heard.

Daniel lowered his gaze. "Most of my friends have left town. They finished their classes and went home for the summer. Some will be back in the fall, but...." He sighed, and Wes had a pretty good idea of what had happened. He was willing to guess that Daniel's world had become a lot smaller and Yan's friends had filled the gap.

"It's okay. Why don't you pack some things, then call up one of your friends and vent? You'll feel better." He sat down on the sofa. "I'll sit here and wait for you for a while if you want."

Wes knew the importance of a support group. He'd had his mother and Frankie, his best friend all through high school. College had separated them, and the last he'd heard, Frankie was living in Seattle with a family of his own. They had kept in touch until a few years ago, when Mom had first gotten sick.

"You don't have to do that," Daniel said.

"It's okay." He pulled out his phone. "I can read a little while you take care of yourself." He smiled, and Daniel scratched his head, tilting it to the side, his confusion obvious. Then he shrugged and got his phone.

Wes read and did his best not to listen in while Daniel talked to his friend Peter. He smiled as Daniel cursed out Yan. "Why didn't you say anything?" he heard Peter ask.

"Yeah, he was a real piece of shit, but…." Daniel spent a lot of time listening and thumping around in the bedroom. "I should have picked up on it. Am I such a loser that I couldn't see what he was doing?" That question had Wes tensing, because Daniel was not a loser at all. He was a good man with strong feelings who had been duped and controlled by an asshole. "Okay. … Okay. … Yeah, I work with him, and I'm going to stay in his guest room for a few days."

Wes sighed softly and let some of the tension that he hadn't realized had been building inside him slip away. He couldn't even be sure why he was feeling it, but knowing that Daniel felt better made him feel better.

Daniel brought a small bag out of his room and placed it by the door, the phone still pressed to his ear as he listened. His movements seemed less harried now, and Wes shared a smile with him, then returned to his reading, giving Daniel the illusion of privacy.

"Yeah. … I gave it to him too," Daniel said softly as he returned to his room and closed the door.

Wes set his phone aside, sighing as he continued waiting. When Daniel emerged from the room once more, the call had ended, and he slipped his phone in his pocket. "Thank you."

"Do you feel better?" Wes asked.

"Yeah. Peter asked if I wanted him to come get me," Daniel said. "But he just got a job in Philadelphia, and I don't want him to have to take time off since he just started." Daniel shifted nervously from foot to foot. "Talking to him was a good idea, though. Thanks for suggesting it."

Wes nodded. "Okay, then, what do you want to do now?" He wasn't going to push Daniel or make his decisions for him. That was what Yan had done. Whatever happened, Daniel had to know that he was the one in control of his life.

"Do you really want me to stay with you?" Daniel bit his lower lip.

"Certainly. My mom will love the company." He wasn't sure how things would work out with Daniel in the house, but Wes wasn't going to leave him alone to fend for himself if Yan decided to come back around. "Let's get your things and you can lock up." He waited for Daniel and then carried his suitcase while Daniel locked the door. Wes watched him more than he knew he should. Daniel did something to him that Wes knew was trouble, but the thought of Yan hurting him again sent a wave of fear and anger flowing through him. His feelings mattered a hell of a lot less than making Daniel feel safe. That was what was important. The rest, Wes would just have to figure out how to deal with.

Chapter 5

"REVEREND?" DANIEL asked as soon as he walked through the back door of Wes's home. The dog peered around the corner and then approached Wes as if he was his long-lost best friend. "When did this happen? Not that I'm not happy about it. Reverend really warmed up to you."

Daniel knelt down, and Reverend sniffed him, keeping his distance. At least he didn't run away. "Mitchell suggested I try him at home, since Reverend seems to have bonded with me. I think he was just trying to find a home for another dog," Wes added, giving a small laugh.

"Mitchell would never put a dog in a situation he didn't think was right." Daniel watched as Reverend pressed against Wes's leg, as if he'd been afraid Wes was never coming back. "Is your mom in bed?" He didn't want to wake her if she was asleep. "Mitchell told me that she was fighting cancer."

Wes nodded slowly. "She's probably asleep by now."

"I'm not," a female voice rang out from the other room. "Please bring your friend in so I can meet him." Wes motioned, and Daniel followed. Daniel suspected that a study off the living room had been converted into a bedroom.

"Mom, this is Daniel," Wes said softly.

"It's good to meet you, Mrs. Greenwood," Daniel said with a smile. "Though I think we met some time ago at a student/faculty mixer. It was my freshman year at Dickinson, and you gave a talk about not letting go until we'd reached our potential, no matter how hard we had to work to achieve it." He gently shook her hand. "That speech had a real effect on me."

"Daniel is going to be a vet," Wes said.

"Please call me Carol, Daniel. And I'm glad my words meant something to you." She coughed softly before settling back against the pillows. Reverend walked around the bed before jumping up on the other side, keeping Carol between them. Reverend didn't seem to have any trouble with Wes's mother, so Daniel figured it had been men who'd treated him badly. "I'm hoping to return to the classroom in the fall, but we'll have to see how things go." The determination in her eyes told him that if anyone could do that, it was her.

"Mom," Wes said warningly.

"Don't 'Mom' me. I know my limits, and I can feel myself getting stronger," she admonished. "Now go get your friend something to drink and a snack. Remember your manners."

"Daniel is going to stay in the guest room for a few days," Wes said. "Yan came back. Daniel fought him off, but who knows what he'll try next."

"It wasn't that dramatic," Daniel said, heat rising in his cheeks.

Carol's gaze caught his. "Don't give him any power over you. What you did was a hard thing to do—I know from experience. We managed to get out from under Wes's father's thumb, but it was no easy feat. If you made up your mind to get him out of your life and actually managed to get him to leave, that's something you should be proud of." She seemed to lose steam and settled deeper under the covers. "Wes, go get your friend settled and let me rest a little." She gently patted Reverend's head, and he curled up next to her.

"Come on. I'll show you the room upstairs," Wes said.

Daniel left the room and followed Wes up to the first room on the right. It was bright and cheerful, with floral-patterned wallpaper and a white-painted bed and dresser.

"Thank you." Daniel sat on the side of the bed. "I feel like a baby," he admitted when Wes was about to leave. Wes turned and leaned on the door frame. Daniel liked the way Wes looked at him, as if he might be someone important, instead of as a piece of meat, the way Yan seemed to see him. "I should be able to take care of myself."

"You did," Wes said. "Remember that. You got him out of the apartment." Wes sat next to him. "You stood up to him and made sure he knew that you weren't going to be his doormat." Wes took his hand. "It's going to take some time for you to feel like yourself again, but you will. I know that. Give yourself a chance to process what's happened and to find a little peace."

"Do you think I should talk to someone?" Daniel asked. "I think there's a counselor at the college."

"That's up to you. Whatever you think you need, take it. There is no shame in asking for help." Wes became quiet once again, then added, "It took me a long time to ask for help after Mom kicked my father out and the abuse finally stopped. I kept expecting it." He turned and met Daniel's gaze. "I really thought I deserved what my father did to me. That I had caused it all. That I wasn't good enough, and I should have been able to protect myself and my mom from him."

"But...." That didn't make any sense to Daniel. "He was your father. How were you supposed to protect your mom... or yourself? It was his job to do that, and he was the one who failed."

"I know that now. But I was a kid, and I needed help to work all that out. If you need help to get past Yan...."

Daniel shrugged. "I think what I really need is just for him to be gone for good." And to stay away from guys like Yan. He could feel his heart hardening. He had the crappiest taste in men, and maybe it was best if he just stayed away from dating. Daniel didn't like being alone, and he tended to let his excitement take over and rush into things.

But then he peered deep into Wes's eyes and saw nothing but gentleness and caring. Turning off his heart wasn't the answer. What he needed was to find someone who would take care of it. That was what everyone deserved. Mostly, though, what he needed to do was give himself a chance to heal.

"I don't know if that will happen. But it's possible that he'll move on to someone else. Bullies are cowards at heart, and you did the last thing he expected—you fought back." Wes squeezed his hand and then released it. "Have you had dinner? I can make you a sandwich if you'd like." When Daniel said he hadn't had anything to eat yet, Wes was off downstairs.

Daniel took a deep breath as he watched Wes go, and couldn't help smiling. Something about Wes really appealed to him. He didn't talk a great deal—not like Daniel, who could prattle on for hours—but he listened. And with Daniel, he did talk some. Sure, Wes was a man of few words, but his eyes and his face were so expressive. At least to Daniel. It was refreshing, and maybe what he needed to do was just learn to be quieter.

Yan used to give him the silent treatment. Whenever he was upset about something or didn't want Daniel to do something that Daniel had looked forward to, he'd go silent and distant. That always got under Daniel's skin because most of the time, he had no idea what Yan was angry about. Daniel should have tossed Yan's passive-aggressive butt to the curb the first time he'd pulled that, but he hadn't. At first it was because he'd thought he was in love with Yan, and later, because he'd needed Yan's help to pay the rent.

The rent was still an issue, but he'd figure it out. Things were going to be tight, but he'd be okay if he was careful.

He got up and put his case on the bed, opened it, and laid out his clothes on the chest at the foot of the bed. Then he left the room and returned downstairs, where he found Wes in the kitchen with Reverend sitting near his feet, watching Wes's every movement. "I see what Mitchell meant," Daniel said.

Wes looked down and placed a few bites in Reverend's bowl. "He's a good dog. And he seems to really like Mom. He's not too sure of you, but I'm sure he'll come around." Wes smiled and set a plate with a sandwich and some chips on the table. "I know it's not anything special, but I never was the world's greatest cook."

Daniel sat and ate quietly while Wes got himself a glass of water and joined him at the table. Daniel wanted to ask all kinds of questions, but he forced himself to keep quiet. Wes had to have goals and dreams, but somehow Daniel didn't think he'd want to talk about that right now. Sometimes he seemed so closed off, and at other times, he was as open as anyone he'd ever met.

Daniel found it frustrating, so he ate his sandwich in silence, grateful that he wasn't sitting in that apartment alone... waiting.

Just then, Wes's phone rang. Daniel was relieved for something to break up the silence.

"What? You have to be kidding me. Okay, Daniel and I are on our way." Wes jumped to his feet. "Mitchell needs us. Someone tried to let Raj out of his cage." Wes quickly ran in and told his mom they were leaving. Then Daniel shoved the last bite in his mouth and followed Wes outside.

Daniel jumped into the car, and Wes backed out as soon as his door closed. Fortunately, the road was empty, and he floored it the short distance to the shelter to get there in record time. As soon as he pulled in, Mitchell met the car. "He's gone."

"Who?" Daniel asked.

"Raj. I found blood outside the cage, so I'm assuming that whoever let him out didn't get away unscathed, but we have to find him. I don't know which way he went, but if you drive up this road, I'll go the other way. We have to find him and get him back in the enclosure. If we don't, the authorities will shoot him." Mitchell's voice broke.

"Okay. Let's get out there and look," Daniel said, and Mitchell handed him a floodlight that plugged in to the car's lighter socket. "We'll call you if we see him."

"If you find him, don't get too close, but keep an eye on him. I hate to do it, but I'll tranq him, and then we can get him back in the enclosure." Mitchell's hands shook. "I never thought I'd need to put a lock on a tiger cage, but...."

"Do you think it was any of the men who were here before?" Wes asked.

Mitchell shrugged. "I don't know. It seems like a stretch to me. They were interested in dogs, and as far as I know, they hadn't even noticed Raj. It could have been kids. Raj looks like a big pet, though we all know he isn't." Mitchell looked worried. "Right now I just want him back unharmed."

"Okay. We'll go look," Wes said and pulled out of the drive. Daniel plugged in the light and shone it over the fields as they crept forward. He watched and let Wes drive. Daniel could feel the tension rolling off Wes.

"He's scared and excited at the same time," Wes said softly.

"How do you know?" Daniel asked over his shoulder before turning back to continue searching.

"He's excited because he's free, but the night has sounds that he's not used to. Raj hasn't been out on his own since he was a kit. He was raised by people, and that's where he gets his food from." Wes rolled the windows all the way down, and Daniel leaned out, shining, watching, and listening.

They went a mile from the shelter and continued. Daniel wasn't sure how far Raj could have traveled. Finally he said, "Stop," then listened intently. He'd wasn't sure if he'd heard a noise, and the sound didn't repeat. He shone the light all along the scrub and field, lighting the top of the weeds. "I thought I heard something."

Daniel continued listening, and then Wes slowly continued. He was starting to wonder if this was a pointless search when the sound reached his ears once more—a low chuff that he'd heard Raj make when he was content.

"Over there," Wes said, pointing, and Daniel adjusted the light. A pair of eyes shone back at him from maybe fifty feet away. Daniel pulled out his phone and called Mitchell.

"We have him in sight," Daniel said softly. "He doesn't seem spooked, and he's heading toward the car. We're a little over a mile from the shelter. I suggest you get here fast before your tiger decides he wants to go for a joyride."

Raj drew closer and then settled into the weedy growth, where he rolled around on his back like a giant housecat. God, it was amazing to see him rolling in the grass like a large kitten, just enjoying the fact that he was free.

Daniel glanced at Wes, who watched right along with him, completely enraptured.

"I think this is going to be the closest I will ever come to seeing a tiger in the wild." He was clearly choked up. Daniel knew exactly how he felt. He held the light still, just watching, not making a sound, unable to move as one of the disappearing wonders of nature played in front of his eyes.

Lights grew closer from behind and then blinked out as Mitchell's van drew closer. Daniel didn't move as Wes rolled down the window. "I see him," Mitchell said as he came along the far side.

"It seems a shame to stop him," Daniel said, not looking away from Raj. Soft chuffs and happy growls filled the night, and he so wanted to be able to give Raj something he never could: his freedom. Daniel was tempted to make noise, scare him—anything to make him run, to give him just a few more hours of this. He sighed and said nothing as Mitchell left the window and went around to the front of the car. He used the hood to steady his hands. Daniel kept the light on Raj and knew the second the dart hit home. Raj jumped, spun slightly, and then went down.

"We have maybe half an hour. I didn't want to give him too much this soon after being anesthetized before." He set the tranq gun aside and raced back to the van. He returned with a sturdy blanket. After getting Raj on the blanket and into the van, Daniel jumped in the back with him, lightly petting Raj's side as Mitchell turned the van around and headed back toward the shelter, with Wes following in his car.

Daniel relished the few minutes he had alone with Raj, establishing a connection with the beast. In a way, he felt a lot like Raj. He'd been caged and hadn't known how to break out of it. Now that he had, with Wes's help, he needed to figure out what he was going to do with his freedom.

Raj, on the other hand, could never be truly free. His entire life was going to be in some sort of cage— hopefully a better one than what he had now, but a cage nonetheless. "I'm sorry," Daniel whispered, and Raj's ears twitched. Daniel hoped he had indeed heard him, because he truly was.

He wasn't sure exactly what he was apologizing for. He hadn't been one of the people who had taken Raj away from his mother when he'd been a cub and sent him off to be someone's huge, and too-expensive-to-care-for-properly, pet.

Judging by the change of direction, Mitchell was pulling into the shelter drive. Daniel continued stroking Raj's side, his rough hair flowing under his palms. He tried not to think of the fact that he was petting a tiger, an animal that could rip him apart with one swipe of his claws.

"Is he okay?" Mitchell asked quietly once he'd opened the door.

Daniel nodded, not trusting himself to speak. They lifted the cat up, and Daniel climbed out of the van. Then Wes joined them and they carried Raj over to his enclosure, gently laid him on the ground, and worked the blanket out from under him. Mitchell closed the latch once they were all out, and locked it. "I need to go inside and make a few calls."

"We'll stay here and make sure he wakes up okay," Daniel said, not moving as he watched Raj's chest rise and fall.

"Okay. Call me if…." His voice trailed off, and he hurried away.

"I feel sorry for him," Daniel said quietly. "He'll spend his entire life in a cage…."

Wes sighed. "Some cages are to keep us in and others to keep people out. Raj is safer in there." Wes's voice broke too.

For a while they stood together in silence, the cooling night air surrounding them. Daniel moved closer, and Wes put an arm around him, their warmth combining. Daniel leaned against Wes, letting his strength hold him up. "I just wish there was more I could do for him." He turned to look up into Wes's eyes. Daniel shivered at the intensity that shone back at him from Wes's gaze, drawing him closer. He blinked but found himself almost completely under the man's spell.

Wes licked his lips, and Daniel craned his neck, tension building as he opened his mouth slightly, his heart beating faster, a bubble of warmth forming around him. Time seemed to stand still for a moment, and there was only Wes and him.

A soft chuff intruded, and Wes blinked a few times, his gaze shifting slightly. The sound came again, and Daniel followed Wes's gaze to Raj. Whatever spell had held them was broken.

Daniel swallowed hard and moved away, Wes's heat dissipating with the distance between them.

Disappointment shot through him, combined with relief and confusion. He had wanted Wes to kiss him, but maybe it was better that he hadn't. Daniel was too damned confused about things with Yan, cages, tigers, freedom, and what all of it meant… if anything.

He told himself it was too soon, even as a stab of disappointment zinged through his gut. What if that had been his only chance and it was gone?

Raj lifted his head and, after a minute, tried to stand. He looked a little wobbly, but eventually his stance steadied. "Hey, buddy," Daniel said quietly. "You gave us all a scare, but you're safe again now."

Raj patrolled the edges of his enclosure as if trying to find a way back outside and then sat down. Daniel filled his water bowl, and Raj drank and lay down in the grass. "You know, we could add a whole new section to his enclosure if we were to add fencing right there. It wouldn't take too much, and he'd have a lot more space," Wes said.

"I think Mitchell is hoping to find him a more permanent home where he'll have that," Daniel said. He was going to miss the big guy when he was gone.

The back door to the house opened and the screen slammed shut. Mitchell strode over with Beau and little Jessica. "He okay?" Jessica asked, pointing. "Bad men mean?"

Beau held her hand tightly to keep her from getting too close. "He's not hurt. But they let him out. Papa made sure they won't do it again," he said, and that seemed to satisfy her as she stood next to Beau, holding his hand.

"I'm just glad you two have eagle eyes," Mitchell said.

"It was Daniel. He heard him before we saw him," Wes said with a smile.

Daniel continued watching Raj, letting the rest of the conversation flow around him. "Are you going to be able to find a permanent place for him?"

Mitchell lightly placed his hand on his shoulder. "I'm working on it. There are a number of zoos who are interested in him. One even has a breeding program. But these things take time. They have to make sure they have the money to support him." Mitchell squeezed. "He's a valuable animal, and nothing is going to happen to him. He'll find a good home, hopefully one with a female Sumatran tiger so he'll have a chance to breed." Mitchell paused. "But the thing is… he's a male, so I need to find a place that needs one. Two males will only fight. And therein lies the issue. The zoo that wants him most will need to build a separate enclosure for him since they already have another male. Cincinnati is very interested too, but isn't quite ready to take him yet either."

"Okay." He wasn't really interested in saying goodbye to Raj anytime soon. Somehow Daniel's feelings about Yan had become wrapped up with Raj and his situation. He knew it was dumb, but maybe Raj moving on to find his own place in the world—a happier one with other tigers—would help him do the same.

"Don't worry. He'll have a home here until we can find him a better one," Mitchell said.

"So long as Raj doesn't eat us out of house and home," Beau commented in a half-joking manner. Mitchell's hand slipped away and he moved closer to Beau, whispering to him. Beau added softly, "I know, honey, I do. And I want him to have a home as well, but the tiger eats better than we do and costs more to feed

than all three of us." He and Mitchell stared at one another before Beau wrapped his arms around Mitchell.
"I fell in love with you because you have a heart as big
as the world, so I can't fault you for acting on it. But
I wasn't expecting you to start rescuing tigers. What's
next?" He smirked. "I have to tell you that I absolutely
draw the line at elephants." Beau and Mitchell hugged,
and Daniel took Jessica's hand so they could have a
moment.

"Do you like the tiger?" he asked the toddler.

She nodded, and Daniel smiled at her. She was just
getting to that stage where she was starting to talk well
enough that he could understand her. She was cute as a
button in her little yellow summer dress.

"Come on, sweetie, let's go inside and let Papa
finish up." Beau lifted her, and she went right into his
arms, waving goodbye as he took her back into the
house. Damn, that was what Daniel wanted—a family
like Mitchell's. Yan had told him early on that was what
he wanted too, but likely he'd only told Daniel what
he'd wanted to hear. And Daniel had gone right along
with it.

He took a deep breath and turned back to Raj. It
was time he put that behind him. Yan was out of his life,
and Daniel wasn't going to let him worm his way back
in. It was time for him to move forward.

"Are you ready to go?" Wes asked, and Daniel
nodded. It had been one hell of an exciting day.

"Maybe we can watch a movie or something when
we get back?" he asked. Daniel wasn't sure what Wes
did with his time other than read.

"That would be great." They said good night to
Mitchell and headed to the car. "I don't have any myself, but I think Mom has Prime Video. I bet we can

find something to watch there." Wes stopped him as they got close to the car and smiled. Then he gathered Daniel into his arms, held him closely, and kissed him.

Daniel was shocked and aroused as all hell by the time Wes backed away. Wes smiled and then walked to the other side of the car and got inside.

In a daze, Daniel opened the car door, trying to figure out what had just happened and why. He slid into the seat and closed the door, then automatically pulled on his seat belt. During the entire ride back to the house, Daniel's lips tingled, yet he refused to touch them in case that lessened the sensation. At the house, he got out and wondered if Wes was going to kiss him again, but he simply led the way inside, only adding to Daniel's confusion.

Chapter 6

WES KNEW he needed to go inside. He'd impulsively kissed Daniel, and now he wasn't sure what to do. He was pretty sure Daniel had been about to kiss him when they had been standing together, so when they were alone, he'd impulsively just done it. Daniel had responded, so that wasn't the issue. It was that Daniel made his insides melt—made him feel vulnerable, or at least like he *could* be, and that scared him. Wes needed to be in charge, or at least in control of the situation around him, and in the instant that he'd kissed Daniel, he realized that this situation had the potential to open him up to a ton of uncertainty.

Inside, he waited for Daniel, locked the outside doors, and went to check on his mom while Daniel went upstairs. He didn't say anything, so maybe Daniel was as uncertain about this as Wes was. At least he wouldn't be alone in feeling like he'd just walked into quicksand.

"Is everything okay with the tiger?" his mom asked. She had her reading light on and set her Kindle aside. Reverend looked over her and jumped down off the bed, then came right around for scratches.

"We found him and got him back in the enclosure without too much fuss. Mitchell was afraid we'd have to call the police, and he didn't know how they'd react." Wes had met some officers over the years, and he'd like to think that they would have been helpful, but the way things had played out was the best outcome as far as he was concerned. Raj was back in his enclosure, and no one had been hurt—other than possibly the person who'd let him out. Wes secretly hoped he got a major infection from the scratch he'd probably gotten from the tiger's claws. "How was Reverend?"

"He was such a good boy," his mom said. "Did a real good job keeping me company."

"Good. I need to let him out, and then Daniel and I are going to watch a movie." He left her alone to rest and took Reverend outside on a leash to do his business. By the time he returned, Daniel was sitting awkwardly on the sofa, his left leg bouncing. Wes knew he was responsible for that, and he let Reverend loose before taking a seat near Daniel.

He didn't sit too close, because he had already written Daniel a check that he wasn't sure he could cash. Not that he had made promises of a carnal nature or pledged his everlasting love, but the kiss had been…. Well, Wes didn't quite have words. And while he may not fill the room by talking, he was rarely without words to express what he meant. Many times, he chose not to, but tonight, he was at a loss. And somehow, he knew that all the words in all the books he had read would somehow come up short.

"Is this one okay?" Daniel asked stiffly.

Wes wanted to sigh because he knew that Daniel's confusion was his fault. He should have just kept his impulsive lips to himself. Fuck. He'd liked the kiss, and part of him wanted more. And that part was big and getting bigger the more he thought about it. But this was something he needed to nip in the bud. Every relationship he'd ever had, except the one with his mom, had gone to shit. Why would Daniel be any different?

"Sure. I like superhero movies," Wes answered as Daniel keyed up one of the Thor movies. He hadn't watched it yet, but it took him about half an hour before he recognized *Thor: Ragnarok* as a retelling of Wagner's *Götterdämmerung*, the *Twilight of the Gods*. Still, he enjoyed it and was eventually able to relax.

"Wes," Daniel said as the credits rolled on the screen, "can we talk about what happened?"

Wes bit his lower lip. "If you want."

Daniel pulled his leg up and turned toward him on the sofa. "Don't you think I deserve some kind of explanation? You kiss me with enough oomph to curl my hair and then pull away and say nothing about it. What's the deal? And don't you dare tell me it was a mistake or some shit like that." He leaned forward. "I know you freaked yourself out a little bit, but hiding your head in the sand isn't going to help either of us."

"You didn't?" Wes's mother said as she came out of her room, walking slowly toward her favorite chair and grabbing hold of the back of it.

"Mom," he told her softly. "Your timing, as usual, is just spectacular." He rolled his eyes, and Daniel snickered.

"Talking about what you feel is not a sign of weakness, and neither is sharing a part of yourself you never talk about." She gently patted his shoulder. "I'll leave you boys to talk after I get something to drink." She slowly went to the kitchen and then returned to her room, giving him a hint of the mother's evil eye before leaving the room. "Come on, Reverend. Let's go to bed." The dog looked at Wes, and Wes stroked his head.

"Go on," Wes told him, and Reverend jumped down and followed his mother to her room. Once he and Daniel were alone, Wes knew he wasn't going to be able to stall any longer. A cold sweat broke out behind his neck and ran down his spine. Thinking about what he felt was one thing—that made him reasonably self-aware. But talking about it was something he wasn't sure he was ready to do.

"I take it this is about as pleasant as oral surgery," Daniel said.

Wes nodded. "I'd rather have my jaw drilled without anesthesia, but this is something I started, and I need to deal with it." He sat forward, his back rigid. "I don't know where to begin, so I'm going to try to give you the condensed version. I kissed you because I was impulsive, something I haven't been in a long time. I like to be in control of myself, to understand the people and things in my life. That allows me to know what's coming."

"Everyone likes to have control of their lives. But most of us don't get it. There are too many things in the world that strip it away from us."

He knew that was true. "There were far too many things I couldn't control in my past. My father's drinking and his temper were among the biggest. Hiding didn't work, and neither did trying to stay out of his way. See, when he got drunk, he got ideas in his head that wouldn't go away, and he was determined to make me understand that his way was the only way things should happen. If I showed any fear, he would yell at me, telling me I had to be more of a man. But that only

made me more afraid of him. It was a vicious cycle."
He drew himself up short and figured he had said way
more than enough. Hell, probably more than he intended, but he just felt comfortable around Daniel, who listened to him the way few people ever had.

"You know it's okay to say what you're feeling.
You don't need to keep it bottled up." Daniel wasn't
in a hurry, and his eyes seemed so gentle and attentive.
Daniel usually was so full of energy, but at this moment
he was still and caring.

And Wes found himself with more to say. "I wasn't
strong enough, fast enough, or good enough, and he'd
make me pay. Make Mom and me both pay. I know
that's where things started, and from then on, whenever
I let anyone else in…. Let's just say that things don't
usually go well. So I figured a while ago that I should
just learn to be content on my own." He swallowed
hard. "Even though things did get better when Mom
left him and got us both out from under him, it's still
hard to trust that things won't go to shit."

"Sounds lonely," Daniel commented softly. "I
know the temptation. After the veritable parade of loser
exes before him, it would be easy for me to feel the
same." But Daniel had too much energy to let things
keep him down. That was part of what drew him to
Daniel. Wes was naturally quiet, and his father had only
reinforced it.

Wes found himself nodding. "So you understand."
He breathed a sigh of relief.

"Oh, I think I get the reason why the idea might
sound good. But there's something missing, and there
always will be." He leaned closer, the temperature in
the room rising by the second. "I remember that kiss
and how it made me feel. It was just a kiss, one… and

yet my heart beat faster and my mind raced. I wasn't thinking of dogs or missing tigers…. Hell, I almost forgot how to breathe. All I could thing about was that small area of skin where your lips had touched mine. It shouldn't be that big a deal. It was only a kiss. Except it was so much more than that… and you know it."

Wes squirmed at the way Daniel seemed to see right through him. It was frightening. "How do you know I felt it too?" He had to do something to get Daniel to back off.

Daniel smiled. "Because it freaked you out. If that kiss hadn't meant anything to you, then you wouldn't be sitting here on the sofa, looking for a hole to crawl into. What is it you're afraid of? You stood up to my asshole ex-boyfriend and you stand outside a cage every day and have some sort of weird staring contest with a Sumatran tiger. And a kiss freaks you out?" Daniel's mirth at the situation was rather disarming. "Do you think that after one kiss, I'm going to get an attack of the vapors and insist that you marry me for impugning my virtue?" Daniel batted his eyes as he spoke in a terribly fake accent, fanning himself.

"When you put it like that…."

"Think about it. You can go through life alone if you want, and you could be perfectly happy. But you'll be missing out on a lot. Friendship, compassion… love."

Wes rolled his eyes. "I can get all of that from Reverend."

Daniel choked out a chuckle. "Okay, then how about passion? And don't tell me you can get that from a dog too, because that's kind of sick."

"Smartass," Wes retorted, but he knew Daniel was right. In his head, it was easy to understand, but his heart had been shut off for quite a while. His father's treatment had forced him to close himself off out of sheer self-preservation. The thing was, he wanted to open up on some level; he was sure of it. The kiss was proof of old, pushed-down impulses rising to the surface, willing him forward.

"That's good to hear." Daniel slid closer on the sofa. "There's nothing to be afraid of. I'm not a serial killer, and I don't go around hurting people. I'm just another guy, like you."

Wes wasn't completely sure of that. Maybe Daniel had some kind of superpower. Maybe he was the antithesis of who Wes was—his kryptonite, because Wes sure didn't seem to have any defenses when it came to him. With a gaze, Daniel had the ability to raise his blood pressure in the best way possible.

Daniel stood up. "It's been a weird long day, and I have to be in to the clinic early in the morning so I can check on the tortoise. Thankfully Mitchell found homes for both of the snakes, so there are fewer creatures to care for. I was thinking that I might take Tommy myself, but who knows."

"Tommy?"

"The tortoise," Daniel said. "That's what I named him. He's really interesting and loves lettuce and strawberries. I've been feeding him every day, and the way he charges across his tank when I put food in his dish makes me laugh every time. He's, like, speedy… for a tortoise." Daniel winked. "I'm going to go up to bed. But I'll see you in the morning."

Wes nodded, a little surprised that Daniel didn't push further. But maybe that was what made Daniel so attractive to him—he didn't press him to do anything. And maybe that was just what he needed: someone who would give him a taste and then back away. Wes needed to figure things out in his own time. And lucky for Wes, Daniel seemed to realize that.

WES WOKE up in the middle of the night when Reverend jumped onto his bed and nudged him gently. Wes pushed down the covers, got out of bed, and went downstairs. He put a leash on Reverend and took him outside, where he did his business quickly before heading right back inside. He checked his bowl and drank some water before following Wes upstairs. He jumped onto the bed and settled right down.

"You're a good boy," he said softly.

A creak of the floor caught his attention, and a shadow passed outside the partially open door. Then the water ran in the bathroom. The return trip seemed more halting, and Wes listened when Daniel's steps paused outside his room. "Are you okay?" Wes asked, and Daniel pushed the door open.

"I was. But I had a dream about Yan—I couldn't seem to get away from him." He nervously rubbed behind his neck. "I know it's just a dream, but…." Daniel yawned and slowly turned away.

"Do you have those dreams often?" Wes asked.

Daniel nodded. "I had them even when Yan and I lived together. It was like he was killing my spirit," Daniel said. "It's okay. I'll be fine now." He went back to his room, and Wes lay in his bed, staring at the ceiling, wishing he could make Daniel's bad dreams go away. Wes had had nightmares about his own father for years. They had eventually gone away, thank God, as he had gained more control over his own life.

Reverend whined, and Wes stroked his head, settling the dog as well as himself. Wes knew he needed to get over this somehow—he couldn't let his dad run his life forever.

The guy wasn't even in the area as far as he knew. But in Wes's relationships with other people—hell, even with himself—it felt as if the bastard was still there, looking over his shoulder. And that needed to stop.

There was just one way to make that happen, and that was for Wes to will it and make it so. That meant looking at things differently and opening himself up to others. Of course, that scared the crap out of him, but his mom and Daniel were most likely right. If he didn't, he would probably end up like some twisted and warped version of his father, and he wasn't about to let that happen. Wes needed to let himself live his life, to stop hiding from it. All he had to do was take that first step. He just needed to figure out how.

"HEY, BUSTER, nobody's going to take your dinner away from you," Wes told the terrier as he watched the dog eat like the devil was going to snatch the bowl away. But Wes knew his words wouldn't do any good. The little guy was in rough shape, and Mitchell was doing his best to get him healthy again. Buster had been found in the back of one of the parks. He'd been running wild back there for weeks before someone had caught him and brought the half-starved little dog to Mitchell.

Over the past few days, Wes and Daniel had talked some more, and they had agreed to see what happened. Wes wasn't sure if that was Daniel-speak for "take it slow, but I've got my eye on you." Wes had had plenty to keep him really busy, with the dogs from the hoarder house out of isolation and Buster in isolation. His plan, since the weather was amazing, was to walk the dogs around the property to let them stretch their legs and get some exercise. Buster finished eating and looked up at him for more. Those huge eyes filled with a pleading look that Wes would have given in to if Mitchell hadn't already headed it off.

"How is he doing?" Daniel asked when he came into the shelter.

"Much better. He's eating like a champion and looking for more." Wes lifted the dog into his arms and got wet kisses for his efforts. "How are things with you?" Daniel seemed anxious, and Wes wondered if something else had happened.

"Okay, I guess. I went by my place—no one had been inside, thank God. But one of the neighbors told me that Yan had been by looking for me. I asked them to call the police next time because he had no business being there." He sighed dramatically. "He doesn't know when to give up. I had hoped that if I stayed away, he'd just move on. But that doesn't seem to be the case."

"When did he come by?" Wes set Buster down and gave him a toy to play with.

"Yesterday morning, from what they told me." He turned and watched the other dogs romp and play in the exercise area. "I just want him to go away. I kicked him out and told him I didn't want to see him again. That should be more than enough for any sane person. So why does he keep coming back? What does he think I'm going to do—take a look at him and realize I don't have enough heartache and abuse in my life?" He shook his head and then shrugged. "He needs to figure out how to move on with his life."

"No," Wes said with more force than he intended. "What he needs to learn is that he can't have everything he wants. That people aren't like televisions or other possessions."

Daniel nodded. "Though I really would like to do some creative things with his remote control." There was no humor in his voice. "I know you're right and that I made a mistake letting him into my life. Why couldn't I see through his pretty packaging to the rotten core inside?"

"Well, now we have to make sure that he gets the message that it's a lot easier to walk away than it is to try to see you." Wes gently stepped forward, looking closely at the purple around Daniel's eye. He had a real shiner from his last go-around with Yan, but it had started to fade, which was good. "Maybe we could talk to Mitchell. I'm sure he knows some people."

"What for? Mitchell is great, but I don't want to burden him with this. He has enough on his plate trying to find out who let Raj out. He's been jumpy when he's at the clinic, and that's only a mile or so from the shelter. And Beau told me he checks the locks on the shelter several times before going to bed. Not that I can blame him. After someone was crazy enough to let Raj out of his enclosure, he's wondering what will happen next."

Wes understood that feeling. "Does he have any idea who did it?" Wes spent some time with Mitchell, but not the way Daniel did at the clinic.

"No, not really. Mitchell strengthened the locks on the enclosure, though, just in case it happens again. He's not sure if some kids got in and thought opening the cage was a good idea, or if it was something more sinister. In any case, he and I made sure the enclosure is secure. Nothing's getting in there now."

Wes shrugged. Mitchell and Daniel should not have to work this hard to keep their charges safe. The guys he'd helped chase away came to mind—the ones who'd wanted Reverend and the other dogs. What if letting the tiger loose had simply been a diversion? Then again, who would be crazy enough to mess with a tiger?

He had the feeling that there was something else at play here—something none of them had any idea about yet—and that scared him. He could face a threat he knew about. It was the unknown ones that sent a cold chill up his spine.

"But what if something else is going on? What if whoever did it comes back and instead of letting Raj out, they steal a bunch of the dogs? What if they take Buster here, and…."

"I'm feeling uneasy about it too. How about if you and I do some digging? If we find out anything, we'll take it right to the police," Wes said.

Daniel smiled brightly before setting Buster back in his enclosure, then gave Wes a look that sent the temperature in the barn soaring into triple digits.

"Where do we start?" Daniel asked.

Wes shrugged. "I have no idea. What do I look like, one of the Hardy Boys?" He stifled an eye roll and actually cracked a smile. "Why don't we both give it some thought. Then we can catch up later."

Daniel nodded, then kissed him sweetly, gently, and softly. Not that it mattered, because it was still enough to make Wes's heart skip a beat. "I am at work here…." Not that he wanted Daniel to stop, but this wasn't really the place.

"I know. I'm going to go check on Raj." He smiled again and turned to leave. Wes's gaze followed Daniel's bobbing backside until he disappeared from view. Then and only then did he have the brain power to go back to work.

Chapter 7

DANIEL WAS behind the reception desk at the clinic, checking over the day's appointments and making reminder calls for the next couple of days. Two people sat across from each other in the waiting area—one, the owner of Geist, a white fluffball cat whose ears were back and eyes were blazing, and the other, the dad of Winston, a small terrier mix, who gazed back at the cat with equal malice. If either owner lost control of their pet, there was going to be one hell of a fight, and Daniel couldn't guess which was going to win. Winston was a fighter, but so was the cat.

Mrs. Johnson came out with her bulldog mix, Hoyt, the larger dog paying no attention to the rising tension in the room. Daniel checked her out and processed her payment for the visit. "Thank you. Do you want to make a follow-up appointment?"

"Please."

Daniel maneuvered the system to set it up, arranged for her to get an automatic text message reminder, and thanked her before she left. She went out, and someone else entered just as Geist tried to make a break for it. Winston leaped and Daniel tensed, ready to spring into action. As both owners brought their pets under control, Daniel turned to find Yan standing at the desk.

"What do you want?" he asked softly, suddenly tense. "I don't believe you have an appointment."

"Do I need one to see my boyfriend?" he asked, looking at the people in the waiting area. Damn, he sounded so sweet, and Daniel was having a hard time remaining professionally calm. What he really wanted to do was leap over the desk and beat the crap out of Yan. And he'd been worrying about a catfight.

"I'm not your boyfriend, and I have the black eye to prove it," he said more loudly. A message that Mitchell was ready flashed on the screen, so he sent Geist and her owner back, knowing Mitchell would meet them at the door. "I suggest you get out of here and leave me alone. I never want to see your cheating backside again."

Yan leaned over the counter, his expression darkening. "You know I'll just keep coming around."

"Why?" Daniel asked. "It's over. It was over long ago. So go ruin someone else's life and leave me alone." He pulled out his phone and sent a text to Mitchell, as well as Wes, to let them know that Yan was at the clinic. Though Daniel had remained calm, his heartbeat was out of control.

"But it's not over. And if I don't get what I want, I'll make you and your friends pay." The darkness in his eyes was very real. "You're mine," Yan said as he straightened up.

Yan never liked to lose. Daniel figured it was some sort of ego thing. He had to be the guy doing the dumping.

"No, I'm not. So just go away. And stay there." He waved his hand at him.

Yan's gaze narrowed and his upper lip curled slightly. "I don't have anyplace to go. Up until yesterday when some new friends took me in, I was living out of my truck, wearing dirty clothes, and eating whatever I could find because you kicked me out."

So that was it. Yan didn't care about him, only that he didn't have a place to go. Typical.

"I guess you should have thought of that before bringing some twink home for a little fun."

Mitchell came out from the back just as Wes hurried through the door of the clinic.

"I can have the police here in five minutes," Mitchell said, his gaze blazing as he escorted Yan to the door. "You aren't welcome here. If I ever see you in here again, the police will be called and we'll put a restraining order in place." He closed the door behind Yan and apologized to the last person waiting before returning to the back. On the way, he shared a brief glance with Wes.

Daniel wanted to go right into Wes's arms, but he was at work and had to remain professional. "Thank you for getting here so fast," Daniel said softly, his insides roiling. Now that Yan was gone, he was wrung out as the surge of adrenaline ebbed.

"That guy doesn't know when to quit."

Daniel nodded. "I'm not sure what's worse, him or his cartoon-villain-like threats."

"They may sound cheesy, but don't discount them. He's angry and pissed off that he doesn't have you to control any longer." He squeezed Daniel's shoulder, then stepped back just as a toy poodle and his owner came in.

Mark was a huge man with a Marine haircut and muscles for days. He also had the cold stare down pat.

That is, until he smiled, and then the illusion totally shattered. Mark had gotten little Lucifer at the shelter six months ago, and both dog and human seemed more than happy with each other. "Hey, Mark." Daniel cleared his throat as he returned to the computer. "Just a regular checkup?"

"Yup." He leaned closer. "What happened to you?" He scowled and turned to Wes, narrowing his gaze.

"No, no…. Wes isn't the reason I look like hell. That would be my ex-boyfriend." Daniel couldn't help looking at the door.

"Did you give him what for?" Mark asked. "I think I passed him in the lot. He got into a truck with some rough-looking guys. They had a bunch of stuff in the back of the truck that looked like rusty fencing." Lucifer jumped into Mark's arms, wagging his tail, obviously trying to diffuse some tension.

Daniel nodded. "I gave him worse than he gave me and then kicked the two-timer out. He made threats, though, so Wes came here as backup. Mitchell helped get rid of him too." He smiled, and Wes put a hand on his shoulder again.

"I need to get back to work," Wes said softly. "But if he comes back, just call and I'll be here right away."

Daniel looked away from the computer, catching Wes's soft smile that he knew was meant only for him. He was tempted to lean right in, but he was at work and had to be professional.

"Thanks. I'll stop by the shelter as soon as we close up here." They shared a moment that had Daniel's belly fluttering. Then Wes left the office and Daniel could think once again. He managed to fill in the rest of Lucifer's information.

"You know he isn't going to just go away." Mark pulled Daniel attention away from the records. "If he's gone as far as coming here to bother you, he'll go to even greater lengths. You should be careful and maybe get yourself a dog." Mark grinned at his own humor and then looked down at Lucifer, who put his front paws on Mark's chest and licked his cheek. "Just be careful and watch yourself."

"I'm doing my best," he said, hoping it was enough. Daniel had never thought of Yan as unbalanced. Maybe willful and selfish, but not creepy and unhinged. But maybe he was, and Daniel had been too blind to see it.

"Do you have someone to stay with?" Mark asked. "My girlfriend was having troubles with her ex for a while, but I took care of him." He glowered and would have looked totally menacing except for the fact that Lucifer kept trying to lick his face.

"I'm staying with Wes and his mom. And you know Mitchell." They both did—Mitchell cared for a shelter full of dogs, all his four-legged and slithery pa-tients, as well as the people in his life. That was Mitch-ell's superpower—he nurtured everyone around him.

"Good," Mark said. Just then Mitchell sent out Geist and her owner, and Daniel got to work checking them out and arranging any follow-ups. Then he escort-ed Mark and Lucifer back and went back to making his reminder calls, checking the door every few minutes in case Yan decided to return.

DANIEL SAT ON the sofa in Carol's living room while Wes mowed the lawn. He had offered to help, but Wes had told him to take it easy. He deserved it after the day he'd had.

"How often do you see your mom and dad?" Carol asked with a soft smile. She was tired, but her eyes seemed bright. Daniel liked her already.

"Once a year or so, I guess. Mom is in Pittsburgh, but sometimes it seems like hundreds of miles away. Whenever I visit, she'll push me to get a job near her and start what they see as my life. She and Dad are friends of a sort, especially when it comes to me. Their opinions of my future are one of the things they see eye to eye on. They figure that I got through college and that should be good enough." He shrugged. "You'd think they'd be thrilled that I want to be a vet, but all they see is more schooling." He paused. "They also don't understand that I'm gay. Mom and Dad aren't hostile about it, but I think they keep wondering when I'll wake up and turn normal." He rolled his eyes. His mother had said something to that effect once.

Carol shook her head. "In my opinion, a parent needs to love and nurture their children, not try to make them into something they aren't." She gently patted his hand. "Having goals is a good thing, and you should stick to them. From what Wes has told me, you work hard for the animals in your care. I'm sure you're going to make an amazing vet."

"I've always worked hard."

"But you have to do more than work. What about friends?" Carol asked, tugging her lap blanket a little higher over her legs. "You need to go out and have fun."

Daniel sighed. "A lot of the friends I had growing up are back in Pittsburgh, and the ones I made in college have returned home to their lives. I didn't realize how lonely it would be to stay behind. I know I'll make new friends eventually, but still…. When I took the job at the clinic after graduating, I still had Yan, and I didn't think about how much my life would change." He had always had people around.

"And now you're on your own," Carol said. "That can be difficult for anyone. But I know being alone is a hell of a lot easier than being with someone like Yan. Trust me, I've been where you are. It took me a lot longer than it took you to find the strength to get out." Some of the light in her eyes dimmed. "But I got out and made a better life for Wes and myself... and you will too."

Daniel nodded. "I was lucky." He'd met Wes at just the right time, it seemed. Mitchell would have helped—Daniel was sure of that—but with the clinic, the shelter, and Raj, he had enough to worry about. Wes had been there when Daniel had needed him, and now Daniel understood where Wes's fortitude came from. There was steel inside Carol that no disease could beat. "I knew I needed to get away from Yan, but I just couldn't quite seem to do it on my own."

Carol leaned forward. "We all need help sometimes. I had a friend, Stephanie, who helped me get away from Wes's father. I had to make the decision to leave him, but like you, I couldn't do it on my own. Stephanie gave me the push and support I needed to go." Her eyes seemed less bright. "I don't talk about this much. It's still painful because my weakness hurt Wes, and I'll never forgive myself for that." She took Daniel's hand with more strength than he expected. "I know the courage it takes to do what you did. It isn't always easy, but you're much better off." She released his hand and yawned, leaning back in her chair.

"Thank you," Daniel said as she tugged her blanket upward a little more.

"You're welcome," she told him, getting comfortable in the chair. "I know it can be hard not to take what happened into your next relationship…." She opened her eyes. "And I know I'm sick and all."

"But you'll hunt me down if I hurt Wes," Daniel said, and Carol smiled.

"You bet your ass." She snuggled under the blanket, and Daniel quietly got up and left the room to let her rest.

LATER THAT evening, Wes asked, "What's wrong?" His mom had joined them for dinner but had returned to her room early. Reverend kept her company part of the time but had joined them on the sofa a little while ago. "You've been distracted."

"Nothing more than usual," Daniel answered. "I hate that Yan came to the clinic today—he always makes me crazy. I stood up to him, and that's only going to make him madder." He bit his lower lip.

"You need to stop that. Don't let him have that kind of control," Wes said. Daniel knew he was right, but it was a lot easier said than done.

He'd been with Yan for almost two years, and at first things had been really good. They'd both been going to school and had some of the same classes. But while Daniel had excelled academically, Yan had struggled. They had done their homework together, and Yan had been super nice and really good-looking. He had these dimples on his cheeks that always made Daniel smile. And he'd let himself fall hard and fast.

Daniel had tried to help Yan academically and had spent hours working with him. But that had only resulted in Yan needing more and more assistance to get through his classes. By that point, the smiles and the easy times together became fewer and farther between. Eventually Yan hadn't been able to cut it at all. He'd dropped out of college and had found a job, but apparently he'd lost most of the money he earned at an online casino. By then, he and Daniel had moved in together, with Yan helping some with the rent and the two of them making it work. At least, that was what Daniel had thought. Looking back, he could see that things had been pretty bad for a while and that Yan had just done a professional job of hiding shit from him. Daniel realized he had let things go on for far too long, but he'd always hoped that the Yan he'd first met was still inside somewhere. He'd been wrong.

"I know." Daniel leaned against Wes. "But it's hard. I really got sucked in, and I'm trying to pull myself out." He wished it was as easy as just saying what he wanted. But he'd allowed Yan to control so much of his life, it was hard to stop. He hadn't realized how much of his time had been spent around Yan and his friends until he'd needed to get out. Then there hadn't been anyone to stand beside him because he'd pretty much let his other relationships slip away.

"And you are." Wes sighed softly. "I know it sounds like I'm trying to pressure you, but I'm not. I don't want to do that. I just want to remind you that you've stood up to him more than once and you'll do it again if you have to. You need to give yourself credit for that." Wes put an arm around him. "And none of us is perfect. I know I'm still messed up—my dad did a real number on me and my mom. It took a long time for me to open up to anyone."

Daniel nodded. "Why me?"

Wes chuckled. "Maybe because you didn't take no for an answer? You went for what you wanted. So do the same thing in reverse with Yan. Go for making sure he goes away." He leaned in closer. "And remember, you're not alone." He closed the gap between them, and Daniel pressed his lips to Wes's, letting the intensity and energy of the moment carry him. When Wes's lips parted for him, he took the opening, tasting Wes deeply as he pressed him back down against the cushions. Reverend jumped down and trotted out of the room, probably to join Wes's mom, but Daniel barely noticed.

Wes tasted warm and slightly spicy from the pizza they'd shared. Daniel loved it and moved nearer to Wes as heat built around them. When Wes's arms closed around him, Daniel did his best to let go of what had been holding him back, hoping Wes would be able to do the same.

Daniel wanted more, and he slid his hand under Wes's shirt, letting his warm, smooth skin flow under his palms. Wes hissed slightly when Daniel found one of his nipples and tweaked it gently. He loved that he could make Wes react that way. Yan always had to be the one in control, and Daniel enjoyed having Wes's pleasure in his hands. They hadn't taken off any of their clothes, and yet this was far more intimate and passionate than he'd felt with Yan. With him, everything had been about ticking off the boxes, whereas with Wes, it was about what made each of them happy. And when he lightly pinched Wes's nipple, Wes made a delightfully low and raspy growl that went right to the depths of Daniel's soul.

His hand shook, and Daniel kissed Wes hard, pouring all the budding emotions that seemed to be taking over his every waking moment into the kiss.

"You know, boys, if you want to do that, there are perfectly acceptable beds upstairs," Wes's mother said.

Daniel jumped and practically landed on his butt on the floor. He felt his cheeks heat all the way to his ears, and damned if Wes didn't have the same expression.

"I thought you were in bed," Wes said, sitting up. Reverend jumped back on the sofa, giving him a look of confusion before settling next to him.

"I was. But your dog came in and pranced around on the bed. Clearly, he was confused about why his favorite person was making out on the sofa," she said with a small laugh as she sat in one of the chairs.

"You need to rest," Wes said.

"I have been resting and sleeping for months. They didn't think I'd live this long, but I'm still here, and I'm actually feeling better. I made an appointment for the doctor next week so he can check me over. Ovarian cancer is a tough one to beat, but I always said that I was going to do it. And I'm more hopeful now than ever." She sat back and closed her eyes. "For now, I'm going to stop acting like I'm dying and do my best to live again." She seemed happy, and her eyes were clear. Some of the sallowness had left her skin, and her cheeks held a bit of color, though that could be because she'd caught them making out.

"Okay," Wes said softly. "But please don't overdo it."

"I won't if you won't." She winked, and Wes rolled his eyes. Then she yawned and rested her head back. Daniel sat in silence as Reverend lifted his head as if wondering what was going on. Wes sat back, and Daniel couldn't help thinking that he was getting a glimpse of the life Wes had been leading. No wonder he didn't often say very much. He'd gotten used to a world of solitude.

After he saw that Carol was asleep, Daniel stood and took Wes's hand, then led him over to the stairs, with Reverend following. Wes turned out the main lights, leaving one burning in the corner. In near silence, they went up the stairs and down to Wes's room.

"Are you sure this is what you want?" Wes asked. "I...."

Daniel pressed Wes to his door with a kiss that left both of them breathless. "I know I'm ready, but I don't think you are." He could feel Wes's reluctance, and that was fine. It wasn't like he was going to jump the guy. A little earlier he'd been more than ready to go. But then... maybe a little time was what Daniel needed as well.

"No. I think it's you who isn't ready." Wes put his hands on Daniel's shoulders. "You just got out of a relationship that was pretty bad, from what I've seen. It isn't wrong to take some time and give yourself a chance to breathe." He drew closer. "I'm not going anywhere. And I don't want you to think you need to do this to please me."

Daniel could see that in Wes's eyes, and some of the anxiety he'd been feeling over Yan seemed to slip away, at least for now. But what Wes didn't understand was that Daniel really needed to figure out how put Yan behind him.

Daniel sighed. Maybe Wes was right. Maybe he had been rushing in because he wanted to get Yan out of his system. He had made the mistake of jumping into bed too soon before, especially with Yan. If he wanted different results now, he needed to stop acting the same way. And if he was going to be with Wes, it should be because he wanted him and needed him, not because he wanted to erase his memories of Yan. "I should really go to bed," he said, feeling a little embarrassed and stupid.

Wes nodded, and Daniel went into the room he'd been using and closed the door, instantly wishing he had just gone with it and followed Wes. Daniel was alone in the room, and he felt alone in the world. Yes, Wes was just down the hall and Carol was downstairs, but at the moment he didn't have a boyfriend and....

Daniel groaned as he sat on the bed, holding his head in his hands. This had to be why he'd stayed with Yan for so long. He had so much trouble being alone. Wes was right—if he was going to be any use to anyone, he needed to take his life in his own hands. Standing up to Yan was one thing. Now he needed to find a way forward... on his own.

He got ready for bed and quietly slipped across the hall to use the bathroom. Then he returned to the bedroom and slid under the covers, leaving the door slightly ajar for a little air. The house grew completely quiet, and Daniel stared up at the ceiling, alone with his thoughts. Maybe it was time he returned to his apartment to figure things out on his own. He loved having Wes nearby as backup, and Daniel knew he'd be there for him if Daniel needed him. Maybe that was what gave him the strength to think about going back. Or maybe it was simply time and this was part of standing on his own two feet.

A soft thunk reached his ears, followed by the sound of nails on the wooden floor. He turned toward the sound as the door bumped open. Reverend stood in the doorway, peering in. Daniel extended his hand, and Reverend approached. He nudged Daniel's hand with his head before he turned and left the room once more. Daniel figured he was taking inventory, making sure everyone was where they were supposed to be, because he heard him descend the stairs and, after a few minutes, come back, presumably returning to Wes's room.

Daniel sighed and rolled over, but sleep wasn't coming. All he did was stare at the open door.

A few minutes later, Wes appeared at his bedroom door.

"I couldn't sleep and heard you moving around. Thinking of possibilities?" Wes asked, as if he knew what Daniel was pondering.

"Yes," Daniel answered as Reverend padded in and jumped onto the bed. He curled up at the bottom corner and tucked his nose into his hind legs. "I take it he's been restless too."

Wes nodded and slowly entered the room in a pair of loose pants and a T-shirt that hugged him just enough to whet Daniel's appetite. He'd gotten a chance to feel what was under that shirt for a short time, but his imagination had still had to fill in a few gaps. Wes's narrow hips and wide shoulders offered him a glimpse of the fit man under the clothes. "I...." He sat up, the bedding falling away from his bare chest.

Wes sat down the mattress. "I keep thinking about you, but I don't know how to say what I need to." He lowered his gaze to the floor. "I don't want you to think I'm not interested, but...."

Daniel waited and let Wes gather his thoughts. He needed to be patient and was doing his best.

"You just got out of things with Yan, and I don't want to act like him."

"I don't think that's who you are." The way Wes was acting was the exact opposite of Yan. He would have pushed to get what he wanted until he wore Daniel down. And maybe that had actually been how Daniel had been acting with Wes.

"Maybe. But you deserve better than someone like that."

Daniel nodded. "And maybe what I deserve is someone like you." He took Wes's hand, lightly stroking his fingers before running his over Wes's palm. He loved the way Wes's hands felt on his fingers. "You know, I'm starting to think that we all deserve someone like you." He leaned against Wes, and Wes slipped his arm around him and held Daniel to him. "Sometimes you will sit so quietly and just let me do all the talking, and I wonder if maybe I'm talking just to fill the space, and then…."

Wes turned, smiled, and put his fingers to Daniel's lips. Daniel quieted and let Wes just hold him as the silence of the house and Wes's warmth worked their magic. Daniel was beginning to see the beauty in quiet.

Reverend huffed and snuffled as he slept, and Daniel found himself growing more relaxed as sleep sneaked up on him. Wes loosened his hold, and slowly Daniel lay down, with Wes covering him up. He intended to close his eyes for only a few seconds, but sleep overtook him instantly. He wasn't sure if the kiss was real or part of a dream, but he chose to believe it was real, even if when he woke in the morning, the only proof of their conversation was a few dog hairs on the blanket at the foot of the bed.

Chapter 8

"MITCHELL?" WES called as soon as he got to the shelter. He heard him working with the dogs. "Did you see that truck down the street?"

Mitchell looked up from where he was moving the last of the dogs out of quarantine and into the main area with the others. "No. Why?" He set down Rufus in the play area, and the dog hurried over to romp with the others.

"I passed it on the side of the road. Two guys were just sitting inside, talking. They didn't seem to notice me as I walked by them, but I couldn't help noticing they had a bunch of dog crates in the back. It seemed strange. At first I thought they might be dropping some dogs off at the shelter, but they were all empty as far as I could see."

Mitchell paused. "I had a patient the other day—a huge guy, has a tiny dog named Lucifer—tell me that Yan left in a truck similar to that, the day he came to the clinic and harassed Daniel." He washed his hands and stepped out of the building. Wes did the same, looking around the old barn and out to the road. The black truck was just visible through the trees near the road. As Wes continued to watch, it moved forward and then away.

Beau came out of the house holding Jessica, still in her pajamas. "Hey, Wes, what's going on?"

"That truck," Mitchell said.

"The black one? It's been by a few times since I got up. I saw it out of my office window while I was working before little this snicklefritz woke up." He bounced her a few times before setting Jessica on her feet. She hurried over to Mitchell, who scooped her up for a hug. "I didn't think anything of it. What's the big deal?"

"It's just a feeling," Wes said. "What are they doing out here?"

"Do you think they're the men who were here after the dogs?" Beau asked. "You know, I could ask around. Some of the guys at work are really plugged into what happens in town. I can find out if something is up." He rubbed his eyes, then took Jessica from Mitchell before heading back inside. "Breakfast will be ready in about ten minutes."

"What are we going to do? If these are the same people who let Raj out of his enclosure, then they're dangerous," Wes said softly. "It seems as if they're casing the place."

"But why?" Mitchell asked. "I mean, if they're involved in dogfights, why don't they just get their dogs somewhere else? Why do they have to use my dogs? These are pets. None of them have been raised to fight." He seemed confused and upset. "And why would they want a tiger?" He shook his head and took a deep breath. "I think that maybe we're letting our imaginations get ahead of us. All we have to go on are feelings. If I had something solid, I'd call the police, but what would I tell them now?" Mitchell was becoming more agitated by the second.

Wes couldn't blame him. The thought of Reverend, Bowser, Sweety, or any of the other dogs in the shelter being thrown into a ring where they had to fight for their lives was nearly more than he could stand.

"Maybe they don't want the dogs," Wes answered. "Maybe when they let Raj out, they weren't just being stupid. What if they were trying to take him and didn't know what they were doing?" Wes had no idea why anyone would want a tiger, but the idea struck him, and he just said it out loud.

"Why in the hell would anyone do that?" Mitchell asked, anger washing off him. "Raj would rip them apart. He's a wild animal."

"I don't know. I was just thinking out loud," Wes backtracked.

Mitchell nodded. "I know, I'm sorry. It's just that...." His voice trailed off as they both turned to where Raj prowled the perimeter of his enclosure. Wes had grown to like the tiger very much, and they had a bond, but that didn't mean he wanted to get in the cage with him. Like Mitchell said, he was a wild animal. And wild animals were unpredictable.

Whenever Wes spent time with Raj, he could almost feel his confusion. No wild animal should be kept as a pet. And yet Wes knew Raj couldn't be set loose. He'd never survive. Whoever had raised Raj from a cub certainly hadn't done him a service.

"I'm probably way off the mark," Wes said, trying for calm. But even though the idea was nuts, Wes couldn't help holding on to it. There was something going on—he could feel it in his bones. He just wished he knew what it was.

Mitchell took another deep breath. "I have no idea what's going on. Sometimes people confuse me—I think that's why I like animals. They don't have ulterior motives." He looked around. "Did Daniel come in with you?"

"No. He dropped me off and then went on to the clinic. He said he had to bring some computer records up to date, so he was going to get them finished.

"He does know that the clinic is closed today, right? It's Sunday, and we should all be taking it easy." He smiled. "Please call him and let him know that if he wants to eat, he should get here in five minutes. Otherwise, there might not be any of Beau's pancakes left." He smiled and headed toward the back door.

Wes sent Daniel a message and checked that all the dogs had finished their breakfast before heading inside.

As he sat at the table, he got a message from Daniel that he was on his way, and a few minutes later, his car pulled into the drive. "What's with the dark-colored truck?" he said when he came inside. "It looked like the one Mark said Yan got into when he left the clinic. I didn't see him inside, but it went by pretty fast. Maybe he's decided to stalk me now."

Daniel sat next to Wes, shaking a little. "I'm so tired of him. I wish a pit from hell would open up and swallow him whole."

"When I walked past, I didn't see Yan in the truck," Wes said.

"I wonder who they are, then?" Daniel asked.

"Did it occur to any of you that maybe it might be someone who's simply waiting for one of the neighbors? That it might not have anything to do with us? I know we've had some strange things happen lately, but it could be that you're jumping to conclusions here." Beau put Jessica in a chair and set a yellow plastic plate of cut-up pancake in front of her. She dug in like a champ, using her hands. She was such a cutie. Wes made faces at her, getting smiles in return.

Wes had never thought of himself as a father, but being here had already made him consider possibilities he hadn't thought he could have. Mitchell and Beau had a wonderful life together, and it was obvious they were happy. They wore it on their faces, and it sort of radiated out from them. Jessica was a sweet little girl, and she would never have to worry that one of her daddies was going to start yelling and hitting her, or drink themselves to the point where they couldn't stand up. No, she would never have to worry about that, he thought with a smile.

Lately Wes had been thinking about where his father might be. He hadn't seen him in years. Sometimes he wondered if his dad had ever managed to dry himself out and clean up his life. But most of the time he just hoped he never saw him again. At least then he couldn't disappoint him.

"What's got you angry?" Daniel asked, patting his leg.

Wes hadn't realized that he'd been grinding his teeth at the thought of his father. Okay, so thinking about him was probably not a good idea. He schooled his expression and did his best to push away those thoughts. He returned to eating breakfast, and soon enough, the specter of his father lifted away and he found himself smiling once again as Jessica finished her pancakes and handed the plate, upside down, to Beau.

"Any luck with finding Raj a home?" Daniel asked.

"Quite possibly," Mitchell said. "Apparently the Los Angeles Zoo is looking for a tiger. I sent them pictures, and they said they'll send a representative out to take a look at Raj in a week or so. I'm hopeful they'll be able to take him. I've seen pictures of their enclosure, and it's large, so he'll have a great home with plenty of room. They also have a female that they're hoping he'll be compatible with."

Mitchell seemed relieved, and Wes couldn't blame him. It cost a lot of money to feed a full-grown tiger. As much as he was going to miss the big cat, he knew Raj would be better off in a larger enclosure, with other tigers for company.

"That's great," Daniel said with what sounded like faked sincerity.

"I know you like him. I do too," Mitchell said, clearly picking up on the pervasive mood. Daniel blushed, and Wes thought it adorable. "But he deserves a better place to live than in a cage out near the barn. It's also going to get quite cold here in a few months, and he'd be miserable. But if the zoo takes him, he'll be in sunny LA, getting his tiger tan."

"Tiger tan, tiger tan," Jessica said as clear as a bell, surprising Beau and Mitchell. Wes let himself join in the mirth, making faces at Jessica, who giggled even more. He finished eating and thanked Mitchell and Beau before getting up.

"I have some more things to do with the dogs," he said. Then he left the house and crossed the yard as the truck passed by the drive. This time he stared at it and made sure the people inside knew he'd seen them. The truck sped up, engine screaming as it zoomed away. Wes wished he had thought to get the license plate when he'd passed it. The more he saw it, the more he wondered if it was the same truck he'd seen earlier. But there was no way of knowing now.

"What are you doing when you're done here?" Daniel asked as Wes finished up his work. All the dogs had been fed, so he let some out into the yard to play while he leashed a few others to take them for a walk.

"I hadn't given it much thought. Mom was still asleep when I left, so I was going to check on her and then maybe watch TV or something. Why?"

Daniel bit his lower lip. "I should probably go back to my apartment. I can't glom off you and your mom forever, and I need to find out if Yan is still hanging around."

"We can go together, then, to make sure it's safe enough," Wes said. "I need to take these guys for a walk and let them do their business. Then we can head on over." He had a whole phalanx of dogs that would make any New York dog walker proud. They were all excited as he took them around the yard.

Wes loved all of them. Each one had its own personality, but they all loved to be outside and reveled in the chance to stretch their legs. A few got overly excited, but they eventually calmed, and Wes wondered who was going to wear out first. This task always gave him time to think, and Wes wondered if maybe it was time for him to figure out what he wanted his future to be. Right now, the only thing he knew was that he wanted Daniel in it.

AN HOUR or so later, Wes took Daniel to his apartment, where he parked, then followed Daniel up the stairs to his door. It didn't look like the lock had been tampered with, and when Daniel opened the door, everything looked okay. Not that he'd expected Yan to have the balls to actually break in and give Daniel cause to have him arrested. Wes figured Yan was too smart—and too slimy—to do something like that.

"It seems okay," Daniel breathed as he wandered through his place. "It seems kind of empty. Not that I'm going to miss the asshole, but with his stuff gone…. I guess the place is bigger than I thought." He half smiled.

"Do you want to move back here?" Wes asked. It seemed kind of sterile, with just a few pictures that seemed like they came from a dollar store on the walls. As he looked around, he noticed that there was very little of Daniel's vibrant personality in the space—just a few knickknacks and furniture that had seen better days. It was the home of a transient, and maybe that was what Daniel had intended it to be when he moved in—student housing. Just a place to stay through school and then move on.

Daniel shrugged as he sat on the edge of the sofa. "I don't want to keep imposing on you and your mom, but this place doesn't feel right any longer. It's like Yan is still here somehow." He settled back and closed his eyes. "I should probably just stay here, because the longer I'm away, the harder it's going to be to return. And eventually I have to."

Wes couldn't argue with him, but he liked having Daniel at his place. He had a way of bringing Wes out of his shell and making him want to be part of the human race again, rather than just shutting himself away and taking care of the dogs and his mother. "You know that Mom and I like having you there. I think you make her want to get out of bed." And for that, he was very grateful.

"I don't really know what I should do. Yan found me at work, so it's not like I'm off the grid. If he wants me, he'll find me, and there's nothing I can do about it. Hiding is only delaying the inevitable. But I don't *want* to stay here; I just think I should. I like being around your mom. She's funny."

"She is?" Wes asked.

"Of course. She has a wicked sense of humor. You'd left for work, and I brought her something to drink before driving to the clinic. I came into the room, and she let one rip, then tried to blame the dog. Poor Reverend lifted his head in a 'what was that noise?' sort of way before your mom snickered." Daniel grinned.

"So you and my mother have this inside joke about farts," Wes commented, wondering if the cancer had pushed his college professor mother around the bend. Mom had always been about behaving properly. She'd stressed that people watched her actions, so she made sure to set a good example.

"Sure. Why not? Your mom is a person just like anyone else. Just because she's your mom, that doesn't mean she doesn't fart... or try to blame the dog. I mean that's part of a dog's job, isn't it? To sleep half the time, be a good companion, and take the blame for those silent-and-deadlies." His features grew serious, making Wes wonder about Daniel too. "Besides, if your mom is feeling well enough to blame Reverend for passing gas, that's a good thing."

Wes supposed it was, but he was still worried about her. She had had such a tough time, and the cancer, along with the treatments and surgery, had taken so much out of her. He didn't know if she was strong enough to survive it all. "I'm just scared," Wes said softly, sitting down next to Daniel.

Sometimes those little phrases just came out, and they had the potential to change everything. Three little words—giving voice to the fact that he was afraid of losing her.

He'd never opened up to anyone about that part of himself.

Fear was an ugly emotion. It made a person do things he never would otherwise. But not talking about it only allowed that fear to grow. Wes knew this, and yet it still took a great deal of effort to admit what he felt.

"I know." Daniel took his hand. "I don't have the same fear—but I know what fear looks like. I saw it in the mirror many times before I told them about me. Coming out to them was the hardest thing ever, but I did it, and afterward I wondered what the big deal was. I can't say they took it well, but they're trying to understand. What more can I really ask for? It's not like they always dreamed of having their only son tell them he was gay, or that their daughter would fall in love with another woman." Daniel shrugged. "They do their best. Fear sucks, and it's a thief. It steals the time that we might have."

"Do you see your parents very often?" Wes asked.

"Not really, anymore. Mom is in Pittsburgh and Dad is in Lansing. They both work hard to make ends meet and probably will for the rest of their lives. I was able to go to school at Dickinson because I worked hard to keep my scholarships. That's why I'm taking this year off. There are no more scholarships, and I need to get some money behind me so that when I get into a good vet program, I can afford it. And working for Mitchell gives me experience, which is invaluable." Daniel leaned against his shoulder, and Wes just sat there, enjoying the closeness. "I don't know what I should do."

"About what?" Wes asked, tension making its way into the silence.

"This. It would be so easy to accept your offer," Daniel said softly. "But somehow I have to stand on my own two feet."

That seemed really important to Daniel, and Wes couldn't argue with him, no matter how much he wanted to. The house seemed so much more vibrant with Daniel and his energy there. After Mom had kicked his dad to the curb, he and his mom had gone through the motions of living. Then, slowly, they realized the bastard wasn't coming back, and they got on with it. But his mother's illness had been like a shadow over both of their lives.

Daniel had brought back the light. At least, that was what Daniel did for him. He closed his eyes and tried to think of what was best for Daniel. In the end, he decided it was best to keep quiet and let him come to his own decision. That was what the generous part of him said he should do. But right now, he wasn't feeling all that generous. "And you can't do that with other people around who care about you?" Wes asked softly.

Daniel turned and met his gaze.

Part of Wes wanted to back away from what he'd said. Sure, it had been a clumsy way of expressing his feelings, but he'd said it.

Daniel's eyes sparkled a little and his lips curled upward. Then he drew closer, their gazes intensifying. Finally Daniel closed the last few inches, touching their lips together in an explosion that burst through the dam inside Wes. He deepened the kiss, pressing Daniel back against the cushions, letting him know how much he wanted him. This time his mother wasn't there to interrupt, and Daniel clung to him, tugging at Wes's shirt, determined to pull it off.

He backed away just enough that Daniel was able to get the fabric up and over his head. As it fluttered to the floor, Wes kissed Daniel once again, tugging at his clothes in a frantic need to touch him. To know what he felt like, to connect with him, skin to skin. Shoes clunked to the floor, and they fumbled a couple times and nearly fell, but Wes was too frantic to stop. Daniel vibrated with energy, his hands shaking as the last of their clothes finally fell away.

Daniel was as handsome and sexy as Wes had imagined he'd be. Hell, he was better. His eyes had grown dark and deep, his lips puffy from the kisses. A light wisping of hair colored the center of his chest and then nearly disappeared, to be taken up again in a trail that led to a treasure to be proud of. Wes licked his lips and swallowed hard, leaning over Daniel.

He let his hands do the talking, starting with Daniel's chest, taking him in, mapping his body with his fingers. He wanted to get to know every inch of Daniel with his hands and his lips. Drawing closer, Wes took Daniel's lips. Daniel's arms slid around his back and his hands explored Wes as well. "You don't need to be so careful," Daniel whispered. "I'm not going to break."

Wes gazed into Daniel's blue eyes. "I know that. You're strong. But I don't want to do anything that might remind you of him."

Daniel's lips curled upward. "There's no one else here but us. And I can already tell by the way you touch me and by how you look at me that Yan is long gone." He shook his head. "Yan can't hurt me any longer. He has no hold on me." Daniel kissed him hard, and Wes worried for a second that Daniel might be letting go of Yan only to hold on to him. But then he reminded himself that Daniel was smart enough to know his own mind.

"I won't hurt you on purpose, I promise you that," Wes whispered.

Daniel rolled his eyes. "You know, honey, your sweet talk really needs some work." He bit his lower lip, and Wes smiled back at him. Damn. Daniel could be so adorable, especially with those huge eyes and wild hair. Just looking at him made Wes smile.

"Then why don't you show me how it's done?" Wes countered gently.

Daniel ran his hands over Wes's cheeks, cupping them gently in warmth.

"Okay. Here goes…." He took a deep breath. "You make me feel alive after months of nothing. I was mired in unhappiness, and you made the sun come back out again." Daniel kissed him. "And I don't want that sun to set. I want it to stay so I can bask in the warmth of the way we feel for a long time." Daniel slid his hands around his back, holding him tightly. "I want you, Wes. And this has nothing to do with Yan or anyone else…. Just you."

"But how can you trust me so quickly?" Wes asked.

Once again Daniel had that look on his face. "I thought we were working on our sexy talk. Now try again."

Wes snorted and wished he hadn't.

Daniel laughed softly before kissing him. "You know, on second thought, maybe you should just remain the strong, silent type. That's perfectly okay too. After all, actions speak a heck of a lot louder than words, and…." Daniel trailed off into a deep, guttural groan as Wes slid his fingers around Daniel's long, thick cock and stroked gently. Damn, he loved the way Daniel's eyes almost went black and how his breath quickened. A light sheen of sweat glistened on his skin. Daniel was stunning. He was all sleek and slim, but powerful. At least, that was how he felt to Wes. He kissed Daniel again, harder, adding all the intensity and passion that was building inside him.

When he pressed to Daniel, hip to hip, their cocks sliding past each other, all Wes could do was close his eyes and hold his breath. This was amazing. Before he knew it, he whimpered softly and felt Daniel stiffen under him. Moments blended together as Daniel moaned and came apart beneath him, sending Wes over the edge right after Daniel.

"Oh God," Daniel sighed, still holding him. Wes smiled, resting his head on Daniel's shoulder, not wanting to move, his mind still racing. "That was…," Daniel breathed.

"Yeah," he agreed with a soft smile and a light kiss. "I think we…," he said, but Daniel only held him tighter. Wes lay still, closing his eyes and letting warm happiness and relaxation wash over him. Eventually they'd have to move, but right now they could indulge in a few moments of quiet.

They stayed that way for a while, but eventually it was time to move. After washing up and dressing, Wes sat on the sofa while Daniel moved through the apartment, gathering a few things together in a bag. Wes took that as a sign that he had decided to return with him for a few more days. "What sort of plans do you have for today?" Daniel asked.

"Well, once we get your things in the car, we can head back to the house and get you unpacked. Then I thought that maybe we could head out to one of the state parks. There's a great one just ten minutes away. We could hike the trail to the dam. It's a great walk through the trees."

Daniel sat next to him, tugging down his shirt. Wes nestled close, inhaling Daniel's soft scent. "We can do that." They sat together for a while, resting against one another, before Daniel's energy seemed to get the better of him and he got up. Wes followed, and after getting Daniel's bag, they locked the door and headed out. Wes followed Daniel back to the house, watching to see if anyone followed them, just in case. Before long, Daniel pulled into the drive, where he parked off to the side to allow Wes to park his mom's car in the garage.

"You know, we should take Reverend with us," Daniel said.

Wes nodded and got the dog's leash from behind the back door. He clipped it on, and once Daniel had taken his things up to his room, they went back out to the car. "How about we stop at the shelter?"

"Why?"

"Maybe Buster would like to go for a walk too," he said.

Daniel shook his head. "You're just as bad as Mitchell, you know that?"

"What?" Wes asked sheepishly. "He'll love getting out for a little while, and it will be good for him. He has so much energy, and while I do walk him, I think he needs more than that."

Daniel just smiled. Once Wes was settled in the passenger seat, Daniel drove down to the shelter. They talked to Mitchell, and soon both dogs were strapped into their doggie seat belts in the back seat, and they were on their way.

"IT'S GORGEOUS out here," Daniel said as they walked through the green-canopied woods, the breeze rustling the leaves and refreshing the warm summer air. Reverend almost pranced as they walked, his head up and tail wagging. Buster, in typical Jack Russell terrier fashion, pulled at his leash, attempting to chase leaves and, a few times, something that scurried through the woods. "Just calm down," Daniel told the dog as he tried to make another break for it. But Buster stood alert, practically shaking with the need to race after whatever was out there. "You need to chill." He stopped and petted him, trying to calm him down. Soon enough, Buster's attention shifted to Daniel and they could continue on.

They broke out of the woods at the head of the lake, where water flowed over the severe concrete dam structure. "I wish we could just let them run and play."

"I know." Wes stroked Reverend, who looked at him with those huge, deep eyes. He, too, wished he could let the dogs run for a while. But they didn't dare. Reverend would probably come back, but Buster would take off into the woods and that would be it. "Still, it's a lovely day." He climbed onto one of the concrete abutments and sat on top, looking out over the lake. It was quite a sight. When Daniel joined him, the dogs settled down in the shade together, finally taking a rest. Wes took Daniel's hand as they sat in silence.

"How did you know about this place?" Daniel asked.

Wes shrugged. "I used to come out here when I was a teenager. It was one of the spots I used to hide from Dad. I could ride my bike out here and spend an entire Saturday by myself. Mom told me later that she'd thought I was at a friend's place. But I loved it here. It made me feel safe."

Thank God he'd found this place. It was his escape from the hell his home life had been. Before he'd come across this little piece of paradise, he'd spent all his time trying to hide, to get away, always thinking about how things would be different when he had kids. How many times had he considered running away? Pitching a tent out here in the woods, away from everyone. But in the end, he couldn't leave his mother alone to deal with his father's abuse. "I used to dream when I was out here."

"And you don't anymore?" Daniel bumped his shoulder.

"Not in that way. I used to think about how I was…." He stopped and let out a long breath. "You don't want to hear about this. It was all so wrapped up in the shit with my father."

Wes didn't even like to think about him, but he'd been doing it a bit too much lately. The last time he was in town, he'd thought he'd seen the bastard going into a coffee shop, but when Wes had peered in the windows, he hadn't seen him. It was probably his imagination, but it made him jumpy all the same. The truth was he didn't want to talk about it. Going over those times only brought back the hurt and pain, the utterly broken expression in his mother's eyes.

Daniel just sat there waiting. And for once, the dogs seemed content to stay where they were, sitting on the cool concrete. "You know it's okay to share."

Wes nodded and then shrugged. It didn't really matter. "Nothing will change what happened."

"Maybe not. But sharing makes it lighter." Daniel stayed where he was, his intense blue gaze holding him. "I used to dream of having a house full of animals, all the ones my mom and dad wouldn't let me get. I was going to open a place like Mitchell's and care for all of them. I never envisioned getting close to a tiger, but I'd have hundreds of dogs and cats who'd be all over me when I'd come home after work, showering me with unconditional love. I knew I couldn't change my parents' minds, so I did the next best thing—decided to become a vet."

"And you're well on your way," Wes said. "And you work with the shelter and at the clinic. So in a way, your dreams are coming true. Mine never will. They were just kid dreams anyway, ones that didn't include my father beating me and my mom, or her getting cancer, or… any of the other shit that's happened."

"Okay," Daniel said softly. "I'm sorry I pushed you. I shouldn't have." He jumped down and lifted Buster into his arms, petting him and seeming to use the small dog as a shield.

"It's not your fault I don't know where my life is headed. After I finished school, I took care of Mom, and now that she might be getting better, I need to figure out what I'm going to do next. But I have no idea—I don't know what I want. My goals were all wrapped up in making the bad things stop. And they have. So now I don't quite know where to go from here."

"Then figure it out. You have your future ahead of you, and you get to dream about whole new things," Daniel told him, taking his hand. "You can have whatever you want." He smiled and then set Buster down. The little terrier unleashed a burst of energy that made them both smile. Wes put an arm around Daniel, tugging him next to him.

"I know I have to figure that out. But I thought I had more time. Now that Mom is getting better…." He closed his eyes and sent a silent prayer into the universe that it was really true. "It's time I got on with my life and figured out what I want it to look like."

"So what do you want? You studied literature, so think of something along those lines and go for it. There have to be things you can do. Contact the college placement office. Maybe they can help."

"Maybe. But first I'd like to have a better idea of what I want. In college, I thought a well-rounded education was going to help me, and maybe it still would, if I decide to go for my master's or a PhD. But what kind of job will a degree in literature get me? I could teach, but the thought of facing a room full of teenagers gives me hives." Wes scoffed, and Daniel bumped his shoulder.

"You're funny." He tugged lightly at Buster's leash. "Come on, little guy, let's head back to the car and get you guys some water and treats." They started back along the trail, and this time, thankfully, Buster was calmer. He'd used up most of his energy on the hike out.

When they reached the car, Wes set out bowls of water for both dogs. Once they'd had a drink, he and Daniel got them into the car. Then they all headed back to the house.

But when Daniel made the turn into the drive, Wes leaned forward, wondering at the strange Toyota Camry in front of the garage. Once Daniel came to a stop, Wes tensed. A familiar man got out, turned, and faced the car.

"Do you know him?" Daniel parked his car.

"Yeah, I know him. It's my father." Wes slowly opened the door and got Reverend out of the back seat. Holding his leash, he closed the door and stood near the vehicle. "What are you doing here?" Wes wondered if his mother knew that the man who had made their lives hell had returned.

"I came to see you," he said, approaching. Reverend growled, and his father stopped. "I came because it's been a long time and I was hoping that the two of us could talk." He seemed different from the man Wes remembered, not as big and imposing. Still, Wes didn't want anything to do with him. There was nothing for them to say. "I know things weren't good, but…." His shoulders slouched and he seemed smaller, and maybe weaker, than the way he'd always played out in Wes's memories.

"But I don't want to see you," Wes countered. "Why would I, after the hell you put us through?"

His father nodded. "I don't blame you, and I understand. I've been in recovery for the past three years and haven't had a drink. I've been working to clean up my life and to make amends to the people I've hurt."

Wes didn't particularly care. He headed for the door without a word to his father. He waited for Daniel and Buster before heading inside himself.

"I'm really trying to get my life together and make up for my mistakes," his father added softly.

Wes paused a few seconds to let that sink in. He didn't know if it was true, and for a second, he hesitated before going inside and closing the door.

Chapter 9

DANIEL DIDN'T know what to do. Tension rolled off Wes, and Daniel stood still, afraid to say anything in case Wes went off like a rocket. He released Buster and took his bag up the stairs. Buster followed and jumped onto the bed, his tail going a mile a minute. "You know this is a conspiracy in order to get me to adopt you," he said to the dog.

Buster seemed perfectly in line with that plan. He raced around on the bed before settling into Daniel's lap. He was a great dog, but Daniel wasn't sure he could take care of one. He had to think of life beyond what had been happening lately. Eventually he was going to have to go back to his apartment, and while small dogs were allowed, he worked during the day, and it wasn't fair to leave Buster alone all the time. Mitchell would probably let him bring Buster into the clinic or allow him to stay with the other dogs in the shelter during the day, but still….

He put his things away and returned downstairs, with Buster trailing behind him. The pup obviously wasn't letting Daniel out of his sight.

"He was right out in front of the house, Mom. He said he wanted to talk and that he's been in recovery,"

Daniel heard Wes say as he came in the living room. He
sat next to Wes on the sofa but said nothing, not wanting to interrupt. But he wasn't going anywhere either.
Wes had been there for him with the mess with Yan, and
he was determined to do the same for him.

"I didn't see him, and he didn't knock on the door."

"Does he know you've been sick?" Wes asked.
When Carol shook her head, he added, "I didn't think
so. It looked like he was waiting for someone to come
home." His hand shook, and Daniel placed his own on
top of Wes's. "What do I do? I just want to yell at him
to go away."

Carol nodded. "Yet part of you realizes that he's
your father, and you want some answers. And you're en-
titled to them. We both are." She looked more unsettled
than Daniel had ever seen her as Wes nodded slowly. "I
don't know what to tell you. My feelings toward your
father are clear. If he's in recovery and has gotten himself
together, then I'm pleased for him, but we're done. I have
a life of my own now, and after beating cancer, which I
intend to do, the last thing I need is to have someone like
him barging back into my life. But that's me, not you."

Wes leaned forward. "He scared me for so long.
I used to hide under the bed when he'd start yelling
sometimes. And I made sure I never made a sound as
I moved around the house, in case he heard me and
started yelling again. I don't want to go back to being
like that. And I really don't feel any need to have him
in my life."

"You don't have to," Daniel said to both of them.
"Whatever you feel is right." He squeezed Wes's fingers. "If you want to see him and ask all those questions
you have, then do it. Talk to him and then decide if he
deserves a second chance."

"But…," Wes said.

Daniel turned toward him. "The ball's in your court. You decide where to meet and what questions you want him to answer. You don't have to go alone, and if you decide to walk out, you can. Because this time, you're the one in control. Get what *you* need, and if you decide that you never want to see him again, it's his loss." Daniel gave him a soft smile. "Because that's most definitely true."

Wes returned his smile. "I just don't know." He bit his lower lip.

Carol leaned forward in her chair. "Sweetheart. It isn't going to hurt you to talk to him." She sat back. "You know, I never thought I'd ever see that man again. That was the one good thing about Reginald. Once he was gone, he stayed gone."

A knock sounded on the back door, sending both dogs into a tizzy. Reverend jumped down and raced back, with Buster right behind him. Daniel peered out the back, but there was no one there. He opened the inner door and found a single piece of paper. He picked it up and closed the door once more before locking it.

"It's okay, guys. The bad man is gone, and you did a great job protecting the house." He petted both of them, took the paper to Wes, then sat down once more.

"What is it?" Carol asked.

"His address and phone number," Wes answered. Daniel half expected Wes to tear it up—not that he'd blame him—but instead he folded it and slipped the paper into his pocket. "I don't know what I'm going to do." He looked at Carol and then him. Daniel nodded his understanding.

Wes's life had just taken an unexpected turn, and while Daniel knew what he would do, this wasn't up to him. So though it nearly killed him, Daniel remained quiet. He had expressed his support, and that was all he could do.

"You have to do whatever you think is best for you," Carol said.

"But Mom…."

"This isn't about me. It's about what you want and need," Carol said softly. "Don't think about me or anyone else." She levered herself up, probably to leave the room. Daniel could only imagine how difficult this was for her.

Wes sighed and turned to him. "Would you really go with me if I decide to meet him?"

Daniel nodded. "And a suggestion? Just make sure it's a public place. That way if things go south, you can walk out and let that be the end of it." He knew he was going to be in this same boat with Yan eventually.

"You don't have to decide this now, though," Carol said.

Wes finally began to relax a little. "Is he gone?" he asked.

Daniel got up and looked out the window. "Yes. I think he left after leaving the note," Daniel answered and then sat next to Wes once more. "Do you want me to help with dinner?" he asked Wes.

"I'm not really hungry, so I'm going to go lie down," Carol said.

When Carol left the room, Daniel followed Wes into the kitchen. "We could just have sandwiches, if you want."

Wes shrugged. "You know, there are times when I just want to be able to sit down and eat without having to worry about what to make. Mom did all the cooking when I was growing up, and I miss it. She was so good, and it seems like what I make is just a poor imitation."

"Then how about pasta? You have some jarred sauce in there. We can doctor it up to make it taste better. And it's something other than sandwiches."

Wes seemed relieved, and Daniel got busy. He heated the sauce and added a little more zip to it. Then he got the water started while Wes located the pasta and made a little garlic bread. The dogs gathered around, looking for scraps and anything that might fall to the floor.

"It's great that the two of them get along so well," Daniel said.

"Are you going to take Buster back to the shelter?" Wes asked, putting the pasta into the boiling salted water. Then he got out the plates and silverware and made up a tray he could take in to his mom.

"How can I?" Daniel said with a smile. The little ball of energy had easily worked his way into Daniel's heart. When the pasta was done and the sauce was ready, Daniel tossed them together. Wes didn't give his mom a huge amount, but he took her some garlic bread as well. Then the two of them settled at the kitchen table.

"There's so much going on right now," Wes said softly. "The last thing any of us needed was for him to show up."

"I know. First it's Yan, who won't go away, and then there are the guys sniffing around the shelter, who are a little too interested in our dogs." Daniel shook his head. "As if we'd ever let any of the dogs go with people like them." He took a bite of the pasta. Dang, it was good, with just the right tang of acid from the tomatoes. "Still, I am a little worried that those men might still try something. I can just feel this tension in the air." He tried to stop a shiver but couldn't. The air felt crackly around him, and Daniel wished to hell he knew why.

Wes nodded. "Knowing those guys are watching the place concerns me." He rubbed his jaw as though he were thinking.

"Do you really think someone's after Raj?" Daniel asked. "Mitchell said you'd mentioned that, but I can't understand why someone would do that."

"They'd have to be pretty stupid."

"But someone did let Raj out of his cage," Daniel said, still thinking.

"So maybe I'm not that far off?" Wes asked. "I know. I wish I had some answers too." He chuckled softly. "About everything."

Daniel couldn't help nodding as he munched on the buttery garlic bread. "Mitchell and Beau are supposed to go away this coming weekend," he said, figuring a change of subject was in order. "I'll be looking after any patients that we have in the clinic over the weekend, but if you need help with feeding or anything…."

"Thanks." Wes took a bite of his own bread. Then he swallowed and drank some of his water. "You know, if there are people watching the shelter, they're going to notice that Beau and Mitchell aren't home. I mean, their car won't be out front, and even if they light up the house like a Christmas tree, if someone is staking out the house and shelter…."

Daniel understood what he was saying. "Then they're going to know that no one is home. And if they want to pull anything, there'll likely never be a better time."

"Exactly. There are a lot of things you can do to make a house look lived-in, but anyone watching would see them carry their bags to the car. And the normal clinic hours for that Saturday have been canceled. It wouldn't be hard for someone to put two and two together." Wes sat back in his chair. "We could say something to Mitchell...."

Daniel set down his fork. "No way. He and Beau have been planning this trip with Jessica for months. They're going camping up near the Pennsylvania Grand Canyon. Besides, Mitchell never takes time off. He gives everything to the clinic and the shelter. He and Beau really deserve some time away as a family." He took a drink of water. "It took some convincing on Beau's part to get him to go in the first place."

"I see."

Daniel nodded. "And we don't know for sure that anything will happen. The last thing we want to do is make him jumpy. He would stay home—I know that—and then everyone would be disappointed. I think we should just keep an extra sharp eye on the place. The dogs will need to be walked, and we can spend some time out on the lawn, maybe make a picnic or something. Put on a little show for anyone who might be hanging around."

Wes smiled. "That way they'll know that there's someone here watching the shelter." He grinned, and Daniel had to agree. Buster woofed from his place on the floor, as though he agreed too. Daniel peered down at the little dog sitting next to his chair, watching him, salivating at every bite he took.

"You'll get your own food when we're done," Daniel told him, though his resolve slipped a little as he watched the peppy little guy practically vibrate with excitement.

DANIEL HELPED with the dishes and fed the dogs before he and Wes settled in the living room. Carol was already in bed. "When is your mom's appointment with the doctor?"

"Tuesday. They're going to draw some blood to-morrow for a few tests, and then we'll know if this is a 'last good days' sort of thing or if it's real improvement." Daniel could hear the hope in Wes's voice. He leaned against Wes, enjoying his warmth and closeness. Buster jumped up and settled on the other side of him, and Reverend lay pressed next to Wes. "I've been thinking that maybe I should see my dad, like you said. We could meet at Miseno's for dinner or something. It's a busy place, and if you come too…."

Daniel smiled slightly. "You know I will." Maybe Wes could finally find some peace. After all these years, he deserved it.

Wes turned on the TV and they watched the Cooking Channel for a little while.

"I think it's hilarious that neither of us can cook very well and yet we'll watch others doing it for hours."

"I like the cookie shows," Wes whispered as he reached over to turn out one of the lights.

"You just like the sweet stuff," Daniel commented.

Wes drew closer and kissed him. "That I do," he agreed. "Mom is asleep, so we don't have to worry about being interrupted again."

Wes was so warm, and his breath held a hint of garlic and spices. Daniel liked it and kissed Wes deeper. "Yeah, I know. But maybe we should go upstairs where there's less of an audience?" Both dogs sat watching them from opposite sides of the sofa.

"Good idea."

"How about I take the dogs out for a potty? Then I'll meet you upstairs." Daniel got the leashes, then took the two dogs out into the warm, sultry evening. It was one of those nights when the air hung close and sweat broke out instantly on his forehead just from walking. Daniel thought he could cut off a piece of the air and chew on it, it was so thick. Bugs sounded all around as the dogs sniffed until they found the right spots before taking care of business.

Once they were done, Daniel brought them back inside and made sure they had water. Then he went upstairs and closed Wes's bedroom door to give the two of them a little time alone.

The sight that greeted him took Daniel's breath away. Wes lay on his bed under only a sheet, his chest glistening in the low light. "Damn," Daniel said softly, his mouth going dry. "You make me forget my own name." Wes had him completely captivated.

Wes crooked his finger, and Daniel moved forward without thinking. Wes drew him closer like a moth to a flame, and there was no way he could resist.

"Wes, are you sure about this?" Daniel asked, tugging his shirt over his head. Though the two of them had moved forward together, Wes's initial reticence still worried him. Daniel had to wonder if they were moving too fast. Not that he was complaining in the least, but he didn't want Wes to have any regrets.

"I'm sure." Wes took Daniel's hand and tugged him onto the bed. "I know it's time for me to move on and stop letting my father and my fears run my life." He smiled slightly, his eyes dancing with energy.

"That's good," Daniel said. "But you have to know that this is a big step for both of us." He climbed onto the bed, holding Wes's gaze. "The last person I was with was Yan, and before that I had a series of awful relationship failures. I always jump in too soon, and I don't want a repeat of what I had before. I mean, I want to be with you, but I don't want to make the same mistakes and...." He could feel his mouth running away with him, and he took a deep breath to calm himself. "I want something new, something special." Daniel slipped his hands around the back of Wes's neck. "I want something like what Beau and Mitchell have. A connection like theirs."

Wes held his cheeks. "I want that too. But just wanting it doesn't necessarily mean it will happen."

Daniel looked deep into Wes's eyes, half expecting a "but" or a qualification.

"I don't know what the future will bring, but I do know that I'm not like the other guys you've dated. I know how it feels to be hurt and left behind. I won't do that to you." Wes kept his words soft, but the intensity behind them was powerful. "I know what it's like to be treated as though you're nothing, and I'd *never* do that to you."

Daniel nodded and closed the distance between them. Excitement ricocheted around inside him, building momentum and intensity with each bounce. Daniel held on to Wes to steady himself as the excitement almost became more than he could take. He pressed Wes back against the pillows, kicked off his shoes, and then gasped as Wes worked at his pants. They slipped down his legs, and he kicked them to the foot of the bed.

Damn, he loved the way Wes touched him, every caress only building the pleasure. There had been times at the end of his relationship with Yan when Yan's touch had made him shiver—and not in a good way. Wes's touch was firm and gentle, strong, yet kind. He drew Daniel to him like a magnet. Daniel had no idea why he felt this kind of attraction. Even the dogs gravitated to Wes, and everyone knew they were the best judges of character. And Wes did have a very good heart. Daniel could almost feel it beating under his hand, warm and sure. Wes was as sexy as anyone Daniel had ever met.

He straddled Wes and as the covers slipped lower. "You're naked."

Wes's gaze grew even more intense, and Daniel slipped off the last of his clothes as well before joining him under the sheet. Wes pressed him against the pillows, his weight deliciously pushing Daniel into the mattress. That feeling of being surrounded and held was wonderful, and he slowly bucked his hips upward, his cock sliding along Wes's. God, that was so good, and he moaned softly, holding Wes, desperate for more. His cock throbbed, and Wes kissed him hard, sending them both on a voyage of passion.

"Is this really okay?" Wes asked. "I don't want to squish you."

"You aren't," Daniel whispered. He gripped Wes tighter, encouraging him as he wound his legs around Wes's hips, opening himself. Wes got the idea, caressing down Daniel's side and then along his flanks to his butt. He stroked his cheeks and then slid his fingers between them. Daniel quivered with desire, already going out of his mind.

It was hard for him not to compare this to the times he'd been with Yan, but in reality, there was no comparison. Wes was gentler and a lot less selfish. Yan was all about his own pleasure. But with each touch that drove Daniel wilder by the second, Wes proved he was just as generous with his patience and pleasure as he was with his time and care. It was an eye-opening experience for Daniel, and he was loving every second of it.

"Wes," Daniel whimpered.

"I take it you like this," Wes whispered, lightly teasing at Daniel's opening. Daniel gasped and shook with anticipation as Wes pressed more firmly. "Are you sure this is okay?"

Daniel nodded, meeting Wes's gaze and drawing him down into a kiss. Wes returned the intensity, kissing right back, their energy feeding off each other's. It was a heady experience and one Daniel hoped would go on forever. When Wes broke their kiss, he reached to the side table, and Daniel held still and waited through the fumble and then the rip of foil. Cool slickness pressed to him, and Daniel groaned softly as Wes breached him for the first time. It was intensely amazing, and he gasped as Wes used his fingers to prepare him and drive Daniel to complete distraction. He was fairly sure he was going out of his head by the time Wes pressed into him. Daniel arched his back, hissing softly as the burn quickly gave way to intense pleasure.

His head throbbed, and Daniel inhaled deeply when Wes paused. He forced his muscles to relax, letting his body take Wes in before he started to move.

Their bodies seemed to know each other, and Daniel and Wes moved together easily. He gazed into Wes's dark eyes and let him set the pace, breathing deeply as Wes's cock slid across that place inside that had him seeing stars. Seconds, minutes, hours—they all blended together as time seemed to fly and hold still at the same time. Though maybe it was Daniel who was flying. It was hard for him to tell. All he knew was that Wes's eyes danced as he pressed over him, and Daniel got lost in them and the sensation that washed over him like waves, never seeming to stop, until he could take no more and everything became too much. Release was the only way out, and yet Wes kept pushing him to the edge, only to back away before taking him there again. Finally he tumbled, taking Wes right along with him.

"Hey," Wes said softly as Daniel lay still, his eyes closed. "Did I hurt you?"

Daniel smiled in the dimness of the room. "No. It was wonderful. I just didn't want it to end." He had no choice, though, because everything ended. That, he knew all too well. He gasped as Wes slipped from him, then settled on the bed, holding him tightly, as if he didn't want to let Daniel go.

Daniel had already lost track of time, but his body was making demands, so he slipped out of bed, missing Wes's embrace almost immediately. He went across to the bathroom to use the facilities and wash himself up. When he stepped out, Buster sat outside the door, looking up at him with big, sad "where did you go?" eyes. Daniel sighed and returned to the bedroom to find Wes under the covers and Reverend already curled at the foot of the bed. Buster jumped up and pranced around until he found a spot next to Reverend, settling down as Daniel slipped back into Wes's arms.

"You know, sometimes I get scared when things feel too right," Daniel admitted. Wes lifted his head off the pillow but didn't say anything; he just met Daniel's gaze. "Because when I'm happy, it never seems to last very long. I was happy for a while with Yan. He and I moved in together, and then everything fell apart."

Wes stroked his cheek. "That's because Yan tried to control you and wanted more than you could give. It wasn't your fault, and it had nothing to do with you being happy. He was just a yutz." Wes smiled.

"Oh really?" Daniel asked.

Wes nodded as though he was an expert on the subject. "Anyone who would treat you the way he did has to be a yutz. It's the only explanation." He rested his head on the pillow once more, and Daniel closed his eyes. He couldn't argue with that if he tried, and maybe it was time to just let himself be happy... for as long as it lasted.

Chapter 10

WES'S LEG bounced under the table as he watched the parking lot through the restaurant windows. Daniel placed his hand on his leg. "It's okay," he said gently.

"I know." It felt like a flock of butterflies had taken up residence in his stomach, and he had no idea why. It wasn't as though he was expecting some great revelation from his father. Still, he was going to have dinner with the man whose memory tormented him, even after so much time had passed.

He knew he should simply put his dad—and his dad's hold on him—behind him. Wes had thought he had, but he was realizing now that his father still ruled part of his life, and that needed to end.

"Is that him?" Daniel asked.

Wes nodded as he saw his father round the back of one of the cars in the lot. He took a steadying breath, and from his father's nod, he knew he'd seen him.

"Just remember that this is about you," Daniel said. "Ask him what you need to, and we can go whenever you want." He patted Wes's leg again. "I'm going to be as quiet as I can and let you and him talk."

Wes snickered. "Somehow I can't picture you quiet, but I'm very grateful you're here." Daniel gaped at him. "Sorry, I didn't mean that to sound as bad as it did. You usually hold up the conversation for both of us, and I like that." He bumped Daniel's shoulder. "So say what you want and just be yourself. Please."

Daniel nodded, and they shared a smile as Wes's father strode into the room. Wes thought about standing, but he stayed seated as his father took the seat across from them in the booth.

"Weston," his father said rather formally.

"Father," he greeted, adding as much chill to his voice as he could.

"You used to call me Dad."

Wes tensed. "That was before you drank yourself to oblivion and beat Mom and me." He wasn't going to give an inch.

"Like I told you, I've been sober for three years. I've had a chance to reflect on the things I've done and the people I've hurt."

Wes nodded slowly. "That's good, but I'll have to see that for myself." He sipped his water. "You wanted this meeting, and I'm here."

"And this is…?" his father asked.

"My boyfriend, Daniel. My father, William."

"I thought you and I were going to meet for dinner."

Wes rolled his eyes. "You actually thought I was going to meet you alone? After the way you treated me? No. Daniel came with me as support, and I'm grateful for that." He folded his hands on the table. "So why don't we get around to the reason we're here." He took a deep breath. "We can start with what made you decide to give up drinking."

The server approached the table, and Wes sat back a second to order a Diet Coke. Daniel got a Coke, and his dad, water. When the server hurried away to fetch their drinks, Wes turned back to his father, waiting for an answer.

"It was a couple years after your mom saw sense and kicked me out. It took that long to hit rock bottom, but that's what I did. I had lost my family, my home, my friends. I was living in a tent in the back of one of the parks—if you could call it living. I did just about anything I could think of to get my next drink." He paused, and when the server set down their glasses, he gulped down some water.

They ordered dinner, even though Wes wasn't very hungry, and once the server left the table again, Wes returned his attention to his father.

"Yes, I did everything you're probably thinking of and more," his dad continued. "That was my wake-up call. I needed help, but I had no idea where to get it. I ended up at the Salvation Army because I could get there on foot."

Wes swallowed. "You do know you brought all this on yourself?"

"I do. That was part of the process. I needed to admit that I had a problem and face the fact that I was responsible for my own life. It was my choices that brought me to where I was. I know that now, and I understand it. I lost everything… and it was my own fault." He drank some more water, and Wes felt the first inkling of sympathy. Not that he was going to let that get to him. Wes needed to stay strong. This could all be a sob story to play on his emotions. His father had done it before—Wes had heard plenty of them when he was a kid.

"So why are you back now?" Wes asked. "What do you want from me?" His walls were still high and strong, and he needed them to stay that way.

Daniel lightly squeezed his leg, and some of the tension of the situation slipped away.

"I don't want anything from you. All I wanted was the chance to talk to you. To see you. I know I can't make up for the things I did. But you and your mom deserve some answers, and maybe if you have those, you can… maybe we can…." He seemed to fumble with the words and shifted his gaze to the table. "Maybe there's some way I can make up for it. I know that you don't want me in your life, and I can understand that, after all the things I did. There's no way to change the past. I can see all that now. But if there's a chance you could forgive me, I'd be able to rest a little easier."

Wes sighed. "So now that you're sober, you just want us to just forgive you and then go on like nothing ever happened? One big happy family. Skipping through the flowers."

His father leaned forward. "No. I am sober, but I don't expect anything like that. Your mother doesn't want to see me right now, and I can't blame her for that."

"You talked to her?" Wes asked, his anger building. "She's been ill."

His father nodded. "Yes, she has. But she told me that the doctors say that she's getting better. I have to give her a lot of credit for having the strength to cope with everything these last ten years. I wish I had seen your mother for who she was back then." The food arrived, and he paused until the server left. "But that's my fault as well. Your mother and I agreed to talk again sometime when she feels up to it. I left her my number, and the next move is hers. I won't bother her until she decides if she wants to speak to me."

"So you're just going to back away?" Wes asked. This wasn't the person he knew. His father badgered, bugged, and bullied until he got his way. He never just stepped back and let others take their time.

"Yes. If that's what she wants." His dad took a bite of his pasta and then set down his fork. "And that's what I intend to do for you too. After today, I'm not going to bother you. I lost the right to be your father a long time ago. If we are to have any sort of relationship, it has to be on your terms, not mine." His father ate some more of the pasta.

Wes picked at his food, surprised out of any hunger he might have had.

"What are you doing for work?" Daniel asked quietly. Wes was grateful to him for picking up the conversation.

"I have a job at a warehouse in town. I drive a fork-lift for them. It pays enough that I'm able to take care of myself, and I have a small apartment and a car. It's taken a long time, but I've been able to rebuild my life, piece by piece."

Wes took a bite of his pizza and set the slice back down on his plate. "I know you were drinking a lot, but I have to ask you…. Why did you think you could treat us the way you did? Were we just punching bags to you?" That was something he had often wondered about.

"Everything around me was falling apart, and I thought if I could control one part of my life, things would get better. I was looking for that control with you and your mother. But when it didn't happen, I got angrier, and…." He swallowed and cringed. "I think back on those years all the time and hate myself for it. I had a wife, a son, and I threw them away because of my drinking and my need to be in charge." He paused. "You weren't just punching bags, even though I made you feel that way." He set down the fork and placed his hands on his lap. "Like I said before, you and your mother deserved a lot better than I gave you."

Wes leaned forward, looking into his father's eyes, though he wasn't sure what he was looking for—maybe some indication that he was being truthful, or a light flashing behind them that said LIAR. He didn't see any of those things. Just exhaustion and regret. And maybe that was enough for now.

"Are you living here in town?" Daniel asked.

"I have a place over the antique store downtown. It's nice enough and not too big. The Salvation Army helped me get it, and they have people who stop by every few weeks to make sure I know I'm not alone. I go to AA meetings almost every day and help others who are like me. I no longer blame others for my own mistakes. I made them, and I need to face them." He paused once more. "And I go to church every Sunday. I have people there who have become my friends. I'm starting a new life for myself, but I still need to deal with the mess I made before. And that's part of the reason I'm here." He kept his gaze down at the table and seemed to be thinking.

So Wes had seen him the other day. It hadn't been his imagination. Damn.

Daniel slid closer, and Wes took his hand. "William, what's the rest of the reason you're here?" he asked gently.

"Because I wanted to get to know my son again," he said, this time with tears filling his eyes. "I wanted to see the kind of man he'd become. I wanted to know that he's all right, that he grew up well. And you have." He swallowed and wiped his eyes with his napkin. "I know I was a terrible father." He pulled out his wallet, hands shaking a little, and opened it. Then he rummaged inside and showed Wes an old picture of himself in maybe the third grade. It had yellowed with time and hard treatment, but it was clearly Wes who grinned out from the picture. "This is the only one I have of you. But I carried it with me always. It was a reminder of what I lost and what I needed to try to get back."

Wes took a bite of his pizza and swallowed, using the time as a chance to think. "You have to know that things can never be like they were before. I'm working to build a life of my own, and you are the reason, at least part anyway, why I've been finding it so difficult. I was lucky to meet Daniel. He's a kind, strong person. But he and I have some of the same troubles… at least to a degree." He squeezed Daniel's hand. "And I have to say that he's the reason I'm here today. Because I wanted to be rid of you. I want the memories of being small and so very scared to go away. You don't have any hold on me." God, it felt so good to look at his father and say those words.

They all grew quiet after that little declaration, and Wes thought about asking for a to-go box for his pizza so he could get out of the restaurant.

"What are you doing these days?" his father said, as if Wes hadn't just told him to go to hell. "I saw that you graduated from college with honors." He finished up his garlic bread. "You looked great when you got your degree." Wes narrowed his gaze as his father nodded. "I was there. I stood in the very back, but I was there when my son graduated. I missed your high school graduation, though."

Wes wasn't sure what to say. "I work at a dog shelter. Daniel is going to be a vet, and I help the doctor care for the eighteen dogs he has in his shelter right now. He also has a tortoise and a tiger."

His dad's eyes widened. "A tiger? Really?" He leaned forward, suddenly very interested.

"Someone was keeping it as a pet. Mitchell and I rescued him from a hoarding situation. We're in the process of trying to find him a home."

His father leaned over the table farther. "Are you sure the tiger was just being kept as a pet?" The way he asked the question piqued Wes's interest. His father pulled out his phone and tapped a few times. "Yeah, I knew I'd seen this somewhere." He slid the phone across the table.

"You have to be kidding me," Wes said as he started reading the article. "This is kind of sick." He passed the phone to Daniel. "What the hell?"

"I spent some time in jail for DUI. I'm not proud of it, but it's a fact. When I was in there, one of the other men had been arrested for keeping big cats and other wild animals. The guy had a bear, even. He was in the country and kept them all in a back field. The thing is, he used them for something like that." His father pointed at the picture on his phone.

"Gladiatorial games?" Wes asked. "Like throwing people to the lions?"

"Sort of, yes. Men get into a ring, and they either fight each other or they fight a beast. Like a tiger, a lion, or a bear," his father said. "The guy in the cell was really into it."

"Do people really do that kind of thing?" Daniel asked, eyes wide and blazing in horror. "That's so cruel… twisted, even."

All Wes could think about was how terrible any animal would feel under those conditions. The complete confusion. For a second he thought he might be sick, but he forced himself to be strong. It wouldn't help if he and Daniel fell to pieces.

His father pushed his plate away a little. "Not all of the people are doing it willingly. At least, that's what the guy was saying. But he really seemed to get off on it." He drank the last of his water, and the server took the glass to refill it. "The tiger could have been for something like that."

Oh God, the thought of Raj involved in something like that left him cold. Daniel seemed to shiver and sat rigidly, the fires of indignation burning fill tilt in his gaze.

Then Daniel shook his head, visibly calming himself. If Wes hadn't been watching closely, he might have missed the way a mask of calm forced itself over the anger. "I don't think so. Raj isn't that violent. He's pretty docile." He nudged Wes. "You don't think that the men watching the shelter could be behind that."

"Someone did let him out, but they got hurt in the process," Wes added. "Maybe they were trying to take him for something like that. I mean, dogfighting is one thing, but where else would they get a tiger?"

"I'm not saying that's what's going on, but…," his father said.

Wes knew he and Daniel might be jumping to conclusions, but it would explain a lot. Raj was a wild animal, unpredictable and dangerous. Just letting him out of the cage was one thing, but if they had been trying to take him for something as sick as that….

"You and I will have to tell Mitchell and show him that article," Daniel said. "What if there's something like that going on?"

"People love danger and thrills of all kinds," his father said. "I hope you and your friends can keep the tiger safe. The guy in jail said that sometimes the animals got injured in the ring, and that was when the crowds roared. Though there were times when the people got hurt, and apparently that really got everyone pumped up. It's like the more blood and spectacle...."

"Just like in the real games in Rome. The bloodlust builds on itself." Wes shook his head. Now he really wasn't hungry. Just the thought of someone putting Raj or any of the dogs through something like that turned his stomach. These creatures deserved to chance to live their lives in peace, the same as everyone else. Wes wasn't going to let anything happen to Raj. They would need to watch him more carefully. Hopefully Mitchell would find a home for him soon.

"How old is your information from this guy?" Daniel asked.

His father thought a few seconds. "Probably five years or so. It may not be happening still, but guys like this, they tend to find something that gets them going, and then it builds. They aren't just going to walk away from it. If anything, they'll have had time to come up with something even more intense. The article I showed you was a year or so ago." He asked for more water when the server returned to check on them. "I'd say there's a good chance it's still happening."

Wes tried to think clearly rather than let himself get all wound up. "Where would you find someone who was involved in this kind of thing?"

His father thanked the server when she set another glass of water down in front of him. "You would have to know someone—things like this aren't advertised except in dark places that you have to know about in order to find them. Basically, you have to know someone who's got an in, and then they would invite you. Things like this are pretty closed."

"Like fight club. The number one rule is don't talk about fight club."

His father nodded. "Exactly."

Wes turned to Daniel. "So we need to make sure that Raj is secure and safe. I'm not sure how." Especially with Mitchell and Beau being gone this weekend. Wes could be there most of the day to watch things, but at night, the shelter would be easy pickings.

"We'll figure it out. But we can't tell Mitchell about any of this. If he thought Raj or any of the dogs were in immediate danger, he'd stay home. You know him."

Wes nodded. "Then we'll just have to make sure all the animals are safe." He squeezed Daniel's hand under the table, and the server brought boxes for the leftover food as well as the check. His father paid for the dinner, and Wes thanked him, then said goodbye before going out to the car. He set the food on the back seat and waited for Daniel to get inside.

"That went better than I thought it would."

Wes had to agree. "He said all the right things. But I only wish I knew if they were real or what he thought I wanted to hear." He started the engine and pulled out of the parking space.

"Yeah. But do you feel better?" Daniel asked.

Wes thought about a few things and smiled. "You know, I think I do. I intend to keep him at arm's length, but at least I know he understands that he hurt us." He pulled to a stop at the sign before making a left turn. "I don't know if I'll ever see him again, but I did get some of what I needed."

"Then let yourself be happy. Not all of us get that kind of closure," Daniel said, and Wes knew it was true. He still had a number of unanswered questions, but at least Wes had taken a step forward. Now he just had to wait and see if there would be two steps back.

Chapter 11

THE REST of the week was quiet. Daniel saw Beau and Mitchell off on their trip, assuring them that everything would be fine. Wes was feeding the dogs, and he had the meat to feed Raj. He placed it in the food container and slid it into the enclosure. Raj ambled over and started eating, watching Daniel as he did.

"You definitely don't want to get too close to him." Wes came up behind him and slipped his arms around Daniel's waist.

Daniel leaned back into Wes's embrace. "No. But he eats so daintily. I always expected a tiger to rip at its food, but Raj sort of nibbles at it and takes his time," Daniel observed as Raj swallowed a bite of the meat.

"That's probably because he feels secure enough to know that he's going to be fed again. He doesn't have to fight off other predators." Wes rested his head on his shoulder. It felt wonderful, and Daniel just stood still, enjoying the closeness.

"You know, I've been thinking," Wes said. "It's supposed to be a beautiful night with a nearly full moon. I have a tent in the garage, and we could pitch it right over there. It would be out of sight of the road, so if anyone tried to pull anything while Beau and Mitchell are gone, we'd be here to catch them at it."

Daniel nodded. "I'd really like to find out what these guys are up to. I saw them out on the road just a few days ago. They took off, but it's pretty obvious they want something." He turned around in Wes's arms. "But should we pitch the tent where they can see it, to keep them away, or where they can't, to lure them?"

"I say let's lure them. It gives us the element of surprise, and if nothing happens, then we have a couple nights of camping out." Wes's voice grew deep and a little raspy.

"Are you sure the tent is still in one piece?"

"Yeah. I aired it out last year. I was intending to go camping with some friends from school, but then Mom got sick, so I stayed home." He shrugged, but Daniel knew it was a big deal to him.

"Then let's get the tent set up before it gets too dark," Daniel agreed. They got into his car and headed to Wes's house.

Carol was on the phone when they came in. "Are you sure, Doctor?" she asked, sharing a look with Wes. "My results were that good?" Daniel thought Wes was going to jump out of his skin. "I'm finally turning the corner." She listened some more, and Daniel felt a level of joy in the house that rose by the second. "Thank you so much for not making me wait. I appreciate the call and will see you in a few weeks." She hung up the phone, her eyes brighter than Daniel had ever seen them.

"I take it that was good news," Wes said, sharing a hug with his mom.

"Yes. It seems that the treatments have worked and there is no sign of the cancer. He says that now I need to rest and get stronger. I'm not out of the woods, but he's hopeful the worst is behind us."

Daniel smiled and left the room, letting the two of them celebrate the good news in private. He knew it had been a long road for their small family. Carol and Wes were amazing people, and they deserved something positive.

TWO HOURS later, they were setting up camp. "I was thinking," Daniel said, holding one of the tent poles for Wes. "You seeing your dad has made me wonder if I should call Yan and try to put things to bed."

Wes dropped what he was holding and the entire tent collapsed on itself. "No. He hasn't been around for a week, and the last time we went to your apartment, the neighbor said that he hadn't seen him. Hopefully he's moving on, and you can too. Why stir up trouble?"

Daniel knew he'd have to move back to his apartment soon, though the thought left him a little cold. He liked being around Wes and his mom. He enjoyed their company, and he definitely liked the way he and Wes spent their nights. Wes was hot, and just thinking about the two of them in the dark was enough to get his heart racing.

He looked over as Wes picked up the poles he'd dropped and threaded them through the loops on the tent. Daniel tried not to let himself get all hot and bothered.

"What about Reverend and Buster?" They had spent the past week sleeping at the foot of their bed. It surprised Daniel how easily they all fit together. If he closed his eyes, he could imagine them as a family of sorts. But then he wiped that image away, because every time he allowed himself to think that way, everything went to shit. In his experience, the moment he let himself hope for something, it was the kiss of death.

"We can bring them out here with us if you like. We'll just have to be careful not to let them loose. Neither of them has been with us for very long. We also need to keep them out of sight… just in case our guests show up." The dogs would not be happy at home, but he didn't want to put them in harm's way. Still, they were just going to watch and call the police if anything happened. At least, that was the plan.

"Okay." Daniel fastened the pole end where it was supposed to go, and with a little swearing and muscle, they got the tent up and settled on a level patch of ground. Next, Daniel unloaded the foam pads from the back of the car, then climbed into the tent and laid them out. He followed that with the bedding, and when he was done, the inside looked nice and cozy.

The sun was setting and the world turning purple by the time Wes returned with the dogs. He'd brought a cooler that he set by the door of the tent, and Daniel pulled up a couple of logs that they used as seats, each with a dog next to them. "I can almost imagine being one of the people out west, heading to a new life, when it's like this."

"Except for the mountains and the occasional lights that flicker up there," Wes said.

Daniel rolled his eyes in the growing darkness. "Can't you just let your imagination take over? It's quiet, with no cars, and other people are far away." Raj chuffed just loudly enough to make Daniel smile. "We even have the wild animals nearby, adding menace to the darkness. I know the old pioneers would have built a fire… maybe. That could attract danger, though, so let's just enjoy a quiet night with just us and the stars." He lightly stroked Buster's head.

Wes cleared his throat, and Daniel turned to make sure he was okay. He slipped his hands around the back of Daniel's neck and gently drew him closer. "I don't know any of the constellations or the stars. But the only ones I care about are the ones in my eyes when I look at you." Wes kissed him gently, and Reverend whined before jumping up and licking Daniel's cheek. Apparently he wanted to get in on the kissing too.

"Dude," Daniel said, patting Reverend's head. "I'm a one-man man, and you're crashing my party." He grinned and petted him again, which only had Buster nudging his hand for affection of his own. Daniel laughed and continued stroking Buster as he shifted closer to Wes. "You know, it seems weird just sitting here with nothing else to do. There's no television or internet to keep us entertained." Daniel smiled as the moon shone down on them. "Whatever will we do?"

Wes snorted, and Reverend whined softly while Buster yipped and tensed. "It's okay, guys. That was just me," Wes soothed. "But now I can understand why pioneers had such huge families. There wasn't a lot to do, so they...." Wes drew Daniel closer once more. "Why don't we go into the tent and see if we can't bring on a little of that pioneer spirit?"

"I think we can do that." Daniel lifted Buster and placed him in the tent. He went inside and got settled on the bedding. Reverend joined them, staking out his spot in the middle of the bed.

"Come on, boy. That's our spot." Wes shifted Reverend to the foot of the bedding and then lay on his back.

Just enough light came through the canvas to il-luminate Wes's muscular outline. Daniel zipped the tent closed and opened the screen to let some air inside before lying down next to Wes. Buster and Reverend seemed to have found their comfy spots in the corners and had settled down.

"They're happy," Daniel whispered, scooting closer to Wes before climbing on top of him. "There's something kind of sexy about being in a tiny space like this."

"For one thing, my mother isn't going to decide she wants to come upstairs for the first time in months and knock on the damned door while—" Wes growled, but Daniel cut him off with a kiss. Yeah, that had hap-pened, and it wasn't a moment he wanted to relive. Es-pecially since he had chosen the moment just before Carol knocked on the door to tell Wes exactly what he wanted him to do, and he hadn't been quiet about it. Just remembering was almost enough to kill the mood. Almost. But there were no mothers around right now, and they were alone, just the two of them.

"That may be true, but it's possible that with your usual athleticism, we'll go through the wall of the tent." Daniel loved that Wes had lost some of his inhibitions. And it turned out he was quite limber and pretty amaz-ing in bed, especially once he let himself go.

Wes chuckled and held him tighter. "It may not be the best idea to do that right here." He closed his eyes, breathing deeply.

What Daniel wanted to do was calm things down so they could settle in for the night, but with each in-hale, he caught Wes's rich scent, which had the oppo-site effect.

Wes rolled them on the bedding and pressed Daniel against the padding with his delicious weight. "It's so dark in here, I can barely see you." Wes slipped his hand under Daniel's shirt. "I guess I'll just have to feel my way." He located a nipple and plucked gently.

Daniel quivered and closed his eyes, trying to take it all in. "So, this is your way of doing things without bringing the tent down?" The darkness heightened each sensation, and Wes seemed to know exactly how to touch him.

"Where there's a will, there's a way," Wes countered, drawing Daniel into a kiss. He slid his hands up Daniel's back, bringing his T-shirt along with them and breaking the kiss just long enough to pull it over his head. Daniel tugged at Wes's clothes, the two of them fumbling a little. There was no way to elegantly get your clothes off in a tent that was barely big enough for the two of them and the dogs. But somehow they managed it. Wes's shirt ended up on top of Reverend, who shrugged it off and then lay on top of it like it was a bed. At least that was what it looked like to Daniel. Not that he really gave it much thought now that he had Wes naked and hot above him, his weight pressing down. Daniel loved how solid Wes was. He felt as if nothing bad could ever happen to him as long as Wes was there. He was safe, and Wes was sexy as hell. Trying to see was pretty much useless, so he simply closed his eyes and went with each sensation.

Wes rocked slowly above him, with Daniel holding tight, moving along with Wes in a quiet dance that would have made his eyes cross if he'd been able to see. As it was, his body felt like one live nerve, and he simply went with it, enjoying the pleasure as it washed over him in waves. Pressure built, ebbed, and then built again until Daniel shook with the tension of a million rubber bands all stretched to their limit. He was going to snap at any moment, and yet Wes held him at bay until he was ready to explode.

"What are you doing to me?" Daniel whimpered as Wes pressed to him and paused once again.

"Just doing my best to make you happy," he whispered.

Daniel tugged him closer and kissed him with everything he had left. Then he clamped his eyes closed and let Wes take him to the stars.

Minutes later, Daniel lay on his back, his head clearing from the passion-induced haze that seemed to envelop him whenever he and Wes were together. He was covered in sweat, and he took several deep breaths to slow his heartrate as he stared out the flap opening toward the star-studded sky.

"Daniel…," Wes said, slipping his hand into his. They lay there, still and quiet, holding hands. Daniel was a sticky mess, but he didn't care. All that mattered was where Wes touched him.

He closed his eyes, his breathing finally returning to normal as fatigue washed over him. It had been a long week, and he was ready for some rest. Daniel knew the dogs would alert them if anything happened outside, so he just relaxed, barely noticing as Wes wiped him up.

Cooler evening air slipped into the tent, adding to the need for sleep, and Daniel held Wes's hand tighter and let it overtake him.

THE MORNING broke sunny and already warm by the time Daniel got out from under the covers and pulled on his pants. Wes was still asleep, so he quietly opened the tent and crawled out, leashed Buster and Reverend, and took them for a walk. They seemed happy to be out and stretched their legs, letting off bursts of energy. Buster was his usual energetic self, and it was wonderful to see Reverend happy and playing. He was a far cry from the dog Daniel had first seen in the shelter, afraid of everyone. "You're both good boys, aren't you?" Daniel said, squatting down to dish out affection. Buster did the licky thing, but Reverend just soaked up the attention. "You are both such good boys."

"Is everything okay?" Wes asked, getting out of the tent and stretching his arms over his head. His shirt rode up, giving Daniel a glimpse of his belly.

"It seems to be." Everything was locked down tight, and Raj was where he was supposed to be.

Wes peered out from around the side of the old barn. "It looks like we have company," he said when he returned. "The truck is parked right over there." Wes pointed west and then checked again. "They're leaving. I think they must have thought the place was empty." He shrugged and headed for the shelter with Reverend, while Daniel took Buster to get Raj his breakfast.

Once everyone was fed, they walked all the dogs and played with them. Mitchell had left a list of things to do, and Daniel helped Wes get them finished, including repairs on some of the enclosures.

In the afternoon, Daniel went up the clinic to feed and check on the few patients that had been with them for the weekend, then returned to the shelter. "Everything looks as it should be," Daniel told Wes.

"I know. So why am I nervous as hell?" Wes asked. "This should be no big deal. These are things we do every day, and yet it seems huge because Mitchell isn't here." He sighed. "I guess it's seeing that truck again earlier. Maybe I'm just spooked."

"Yeah." On one hand, Daniel was hoping the guys in the truck would take the bait and try something, but on the other, he didn't. What if he and Wes couldn't stop them? He kept wondering if he should call the police, but what was he going to tell them? That a truck had parked on the side of the road? In his heart, he knew something was off, but it sounded dumb when he put it into words. At least he wasn't here alone.

Daniel smiled as Wes came out of the shelter building with Pinkie, a little poodle, in his arms. She settled right in. Reverend followed, watching Wes carefully, as if he was afraid he was going to be replaced in Wes's affections. "It's okay, boy. You know I'll always love you best." Wes petted him gently, still holding Pinkie.

That was one of the things Daniel loved about Wes. He spent so much time with the other dogs, going above and beyond to make sure that all the animals were cared for and received affection. "Mom sent a message. She said I got call at the house from a college in Shippensburg. I sent out some résumés a few months ago before Mom took a turn for the worse, and she said they want to set up an interview." He was pretty excited.

"That's awesome," Daniel said.

Wes looked around. "But what about all this?"

Daniel lifted Buster and came over to Wes. "You feel for others more than anyone else I know. And you went to school for literature. Maybe you can find a job where you can use both." He slipped closer. "You need to follow your passions. I know you love the dogs, but this is a menial job that isn't going anywhere. Mitchell runs the shelter as a nonprofit. And you can do so much more good somewhere else. I know it."

"I know. But…." He swallowed hard. "My life has been taking care of Mom and then working here. I…. Maybe you're right. I need to follow my passion… all of them. Maybe I could develop a class… literature and the animal kingdom… or something. I don't know. I'll think about it."

Daniel understood. As emotionally difficult as Wes's life had been, he hadn't really stepped outside of the bubble of his small family. "You know, we all need to get out on our own eventually, and that's okay. Kids grow up and move away to build their own life. There's nothing to feel bad about."

"But what will Mom do when I leave?" Wes asked.

"Your mom seems to be improving. I know it's slow, but eventually she'll go back to work and spend time with her friends and restart her career. She's already talking about working on her plans for the fall. I know that may be a little fast, but she's looking ahead, and you need to do the same."

Wes nodded. "I know I need to move on, but I worry about her."

Daniel chuckled softly. "And she worries about you too. So just let yourself get on with your life." He was beginning to wonder if Wes was really ready to step out of his comfortable little bubble. Not that he could blame him. After all the crap he'd gone through with Yan, Daniel had wanted to just curl up in bed with the covers over his head and hide. But Mitchell had been counting on him, and he had to move forward. And he'd had Wes to help him. "You have so much to offer."

Wes's eyes widened. "I do?"

In that one question, Daniel truly understood the insecurity that lurked inside Wes. It had probably always been there but had only been accentuated and nurtured by the way his father had treated him. Daniel wanted to smack Wes's dad upside the head for that. "Of course you do. You work hard and throw yourself into everything you try. So go for it and see what happens. The worst that might happen is that you aren't what they need. But you'll gain some experience anyway.

"You're right." Finally, that smile that Daniel liked so much grew on his lips. He looked around. "What else do we need to do?"

Daniel checked over the list and shrugged. "I think we've done just about everything. Mitchell is going to clear Raj's pen. He may need help to lure him into his den and then lower the separator panel. But he's doing well enough." He set the list aside, and Wes went inside and placed Pinkie back into her enclosure, then shut the door.

The dogs had all been exercised, fed, watered, and given any medication they required. Under normal circumstances, they would go home until they needed to do the final feeding of the day. But Daniel didn't want to leave the shelter unattended in case their friends made an unscheduled appearance.

"Why don't you go back to the house or to your apartment to check on your mail? I can stay here and watch over things for a while."

Daniel grinned. "I was just about to offer the same thing." He bumped Wes's shoulder, and he put his arm around him. "You know, I'm so lucky to have met you." He closed his eyes and leaned his head against Wes's shoulder.

"Me too," Wes whispered. "I figured I was going to spend most of my life taking care of Mom, and then…." He sighed.

"And then this man with huge, dark eyes, few words, and a smile that can rival the sun walked into my life." He leaned closer, and Wes kissed him, sending a shiver through Daniel that he hoped would never end.

DANIEL EVENTUALLY did as Wes suggested. At his apartment, he got the mail and checked things over inside. Everything was as it should be, and he left. But just as he pulled the door closed behind him, Yan strode over to him.

Daniel tensed before he could stop himself.

"I was wondering when you were going to show up."

"I don't have to answer to you."

"No. You just break up with me and then disappear with some other guy. I always knew if I didn't keep a close eye on you, you'd be off with the first guy to come along." He sneered.

Daniel snorted. "I wasn't the one in our bed screwing some other guy. That was you. I don't owe you anything. Now get out of the way."

Yan prowled closer and pressed Daniel against the wall.

Daniel's heart rate skyrocketed, and he wondered what Yan was going to do. If the past was any indication, he wasn't above using his fists.

"Look, you little slut—"

"Go away," Daniel said loudly. "And stop projecting your crap onto me. You were the cheater, and you were the bad boyfriend." He'd had more than enough of Yan's intimidation tactics. "What happened to the guy you were screwing? Did he dump you too?" Damn, there were times when he definitely needed to learn to keep his mouth shut.

"I had to stay with some new friends," Yan snapped, his face growing redder by the second.

"So he did dump your sorry ass, then." There was a certain delight in knowing that.

Yan looked about to blow his top and pulled his arm back. Daniel knew he had gone too far, but it was the truth. "Is hitting all you know how to do?"

Yan sneered and reached into his pocket. This time, though, he pulled out a switchblade.

"You little shit," Yan ground out between his teeth as he snapped the knife open.

Daniel felt the blood drain from his face and knew he had to think fast or he was going to be in a world of hurt. So he attacked, pushing Yan as hard as he could, throwing him off balance just long enough to bring his knee up into Yan's groin with enough force to do some damage.

Yan yelled and grabbed himself, and Daniel pushed him over onto the floor, then ran for the exit.

"I'll get you for this. You'll pay one way or another. Just wait until I get my hands on you and those fucking dogs you love so damned much."

Daniel burst out of the building and ran to his car. As he pulled out, he saw Yan hobble out of the building, with his downstairs neighbor giving Yan an earful.

He drove through town and out to the shelter. Wes met him in the yard with a platoon of dogs on leashes. Obviously he could tell something was wrong by the look on Daniels face. "Was Yan there?"

Daniel nodded. "He backed me in a corner, and I dropped him with a knee to the nuts." He heaved a breath of air. "This time he had a knife."

Wes gasped in concern. "He's escalating. You have to call the police and report him." His words came quickly with maybe a hint of panic. "He didn't hurt you, did he?"

Daniel shook his head. "I'm okay." Then he made the call, finally able to think straight now that he had a little distance from Yan and was with Wes.

"Did anyone else see him?" Wes asked once Daniel assured the officer that he was fine and in a safe place.

Daniel shook his head. "Nope. My neighbor saw him when he came out after me, but he wasn't there before." Suddenly the thought of what might have happened hit him, and he started to shake. "He was watching my place. I'd hoped he had given up, but he seems to be stalking me. I'm really starting to think he's unbalanced."

"Maybe there's something in the water. All of these crazy people are coming out of the woodwork— Yan, my father, the people after the dogs, whoever let Raj out… it's unnerving." Wes sounded as concerned as Daniel felt.

Daniel thought Wes was going to drag him into the tent to check him over personally, from his intensity and the way his eyes darkened. Not that Daniel would have minded. With Yan, that kind of behavior had always seemed creepy, but with Wes, it was different. Daniel knew he cared. Wes wasn't going to force him to do anything he didn't want to do. He just wanted to protect him. There was a huge difference. Daniel appreciated that.

"I'm fine. He didn't hurt me, although I'm sure he would have if I'd given him the chance."

Wes swallowed hard. "Yeah, but next time he'll be more prepared and even more dangerous. It isn't normal for someone to stalk an ex the way he's doing. If he cared for you, why did he have a knife? That's really messed up." Wes pulled him close and held him tight. "We're going to have to be more careful."

"I just thought of something. What if he comes after you?" Daniel asked.

"I don't think he will. Yan seems fixated on you. I mean, he came to the clinic and then staked out the apartment. Yan is checking out places he knows you'll need to be." He sighed, and Daniel tried not to freak out. "I hope the police can do something. Of course, they can issue a restraining order, but do those really help? We'll just have to make sure you're not alone. At least now if he pulls something, the police are already aware of the situation."

Daniel just wanted Yan to back off and leave him alone. But in the meantime, he joined Wes in spending time with the dogs as they waited for the police to arrive.

THERE WAS only so much the police could do since there were no witnesses to Yan's threats, but Carter and Red took his statement and said they would file a report. As Daniel had expected, they suggested a restraining order. "Do you know where he's living?" Red asked.

Daniel shook his head. "He said he was staying with some new friends, but I don't know who they are. I wasn't at my apartment for very long, so he's got to be watching the place."

"Okay. We'll check it out, and when we find him, we'll put the fear of God into him. A lot of times just knowing the police are watching can be enough of a deterrent. And if he shows up again, call right away. Don't try to take him on yourself. Your friend is right."

Red nodded at Wes. "It's likely he is escalating. If he does turn up, it isn't going to be a social call. In the meantime, we'll do our best to find him."

Daniel couldn't ask for more than that. He thanked the officers and watched as they pulled out of the drive.

"You going to be okay?" Wes asked as he hugged him.

Daniel went right into his arms, closed his eyes, and tried not to fall to pieces. He could think straight in the heat of the moment, but now that it was over, all he wanted to do was hide. "I hate this," he said, his voice muffled in Wes's shirt.

"Let's go to the house for a little while. It's just up the way, and we can have something to eat. We'll lock up the shelter and leave the car here so it looks like someone is around. Then we'll come later for the evening feeding and to check on Raj before we go to bed."

It sounded like a good idea, and it would give Daniel a few minutes to think.

They walked the short distance to Wes's house, where they found Carol in the kitchen, sitting at the table, with something delicious-smelling in the oven. "Mom…."

"I needed to do something," she told Wes. "Now wash up and set the table." That was probably something she had said a lot, and Wes seemed to relax at the familiar circumstances.

Daniel helped set the table, and Wes got the baked pasta out of the oven and placed the dish on the table. The scents of garlic, oregano, and spices filled the kitchen, making Daniel's stomach rumble.

Carol served each of them, and they settled down to a nice family-style dinner.

Daniel was grateful Wes didn't talk about what had happened. Carol didn't need that kind of worry. However,

they did discuss what they thought might be happening
with the men in the truck, and what Wes's father had said.

"Do you think we're overreacting?" Daniel asked.
He really wondered if they had been jumping to a million conclusions.

"I don't know. But since Mitchell put you in charge
of the shelter, I'd take that responsibility pretty serious-
ly. And if strange men are hanging around, they must
want something." She set her fork on her plate. "You
two have to promise me that if anything happens, you'll
call the police right away. Don't be heroes, even if these
men are after the dogs or the tiger. Stopping them isn't
worth either of you getting hurt. Do you hear me?" The
motherly snap to her voice was unmistakable.

Wes rolled his eyes and got a sharp look from his
mother.

"I mean it. I know both of you love those animals,
and Reverend and Buster here are really special…." The
dogs' nails clicked on the wood floor as they came over
to her side of the table. "And I'm sure all the others in the
shelter are just as wonderful. But you can't put your lives
in danger. Promise me that if something happens, you'll
call the police and get out of the way. Let them handle
things. Neither one of you is James Bond."

Daniel found himself nodding, and Wes did as well.
This had gone past just a feeling. Carol was right—they
needed help. If they wanted to protect the animals, they
had to get the police involved—or at least some police
advice. Daniel figured he could call Hank and see what
he thought about the situation.

"Just finish your dinner," she added with more than
a hint of exasperation. "And mind what I told you."

"And you need to watch how much you're doing
and not overreach," Wes told her. "I know the doctor

had good news for you when you spoke to him earlier in the week, but that doesn't mean you should wear yourself out."

Carol grinned. "I know. And you know I love you. But if I had to eat one more dinner of sandwiches, I swear my taste buds were going to roll over and die."

Daniel had to admit, she sure seemed to be feeling better. And he was so happy—for her and for Wes.

"And just so you remember, I'm the one who raised you," she said. "And I think I know my own body better than you do." She ate some more of the pasta and then pushed her chair back. Buster jumped into her lap and settled down for some attention. Reverend sat next to her, and Wes snapped his fingers softly. Reverend came over to him, and Wes gently stroked his head while he ate.

Daniel ate slowly, watching and trying not to let himself get pulled too deeply into the notion of how things could be. This scene was enticing. Maybe he could actually have a family with Wes, instead of things going to shit the way they usually did.

Part of him wondered if it would be better for him to simply quit while he was ahead. He could return home, even with the situation with Yan. Wes represented so much more than Yan ever did to Daniel. If things didn't work out between them, it was going to hurt a hell of a lot more than a black eye or a bruise on the arm. The way his feelings for Wes were deepening worried Daniel. If his relationship luck continued the way it had in the past, things should start to go downhill pretty soon. And this time he knew the ending was going to hurt more than it ever had before.

Chapter 12

THE TEMPERATURE fell after sunset and continued to plummet for hours, with a front bringing in cooler and drier air. Daniel must have felt the chill, because he plastered himself against Wes, throwing off a lot of heat and warming up the air inside the tent, which was amazing. In the near pitch blackness, Wes closed the flap to trap in the warmth. Then he slid an arm around Daniel and settled in for sleep. And yet this felt too good to waste, and he wanted to be awake for each second of it. Each time he inhaled, he got a little whiff of Daniel's scent, and his soft snuffles were adorable. He snuggled under the blanket, pulling it a little tighter around them, and closed his eyes as fatigue washed over him. But a soft woof from Reverend heightened his senses.

Wes held his breath, listening intently.

A quiet voice reached his ears. He couldn't tell what was being said, but the whispers carried a sense of urgency. Wes gently shook Daniel awake, motioned him to be quiet, and felt the tension flood into his body.

Daniel sat up and began to dress while Wes did the same, trying to remain as silent as possible.

"There's no one here. The house is dark." The whisper held frustration.

Daniel tapped Wes's arm and then squeezed it hard. Wes stilled, and Daniel leaned close.

"That voice. I know it. It's Yan," he breathed.

Wes had to stop himself from going off like a roman candle.

"We can take whatever dogs you want, along with the tiger. Just back the cage up to the door and we can lure him in with food."

Wes saw red, and Reverend woofed again.

"What was that?" Yan asked.

"Just a dog. There are tons of them here," another voice said. "Just take the strongest dogs you can get. They'll be great for training."

"Go get the truck in here right away," a third voice commanded. Now they were speaking more normally. "I want the dogs and the tiger loaded and out of here before these idiots have a clue what we're doing."

"You're sure this is what Russell wants?" Yan asked.

"Hell yeah," voice number two said. "He's been talking about this for the last week. The tiger will make the games a real blast, and he's been after the dogs ever since that do-gooder vet turned him away. Russell wants to make the guy pay. And the best way to do that is to relieve him of the dogs and the tiger. Russell will be happy, and you'll get even with that ex-boyfriend of yours all at the same time. The guy isn't even going to have a clue that it was you." He chuckled.

"I'll get the truck," voice number three said as the shelter door slid open on its rollers, the familiar sound easily reaching Wes's ears. Shit, these guys were about the enter the shelter, and who the fuck knew what they were prepared to do to those dogs?

Daniel squeezed Wes's arm so hard it hurt as he fumbled around. A light shone, then was suppressed by the bedding as Daniel made a call to the police, urgency filling his soft voice. That was smart, but these guys could be gone by the time the police showed up. And what kind of harm could they do in the meantime?

Wes didn't want to let Reverend go, but as soon as he partially unzipped the tent to get out, Reverend bounded past him, barking and sending up the alarm. Buster joined in, as did the rest of the shelter dogs, raining down one hell of a ruckus. Even Raj got into the act, sending a cry into the night, adding to the cacophony of sound.

"What the hell do you think you're doing?" Wes yelled as loudly as he dared. Fencing rattled and footsteps pounded the ground, receding into the night, with Reverend and Buster continuing to send up the alarm. It was like a treble and bass clef warning system heading off into the distance, with yells and even a scream piercing the darkness. Wes called Reverend and Buster back to him, pleased when the dogs responded. At least neither of them was hurt.

"You guys did so good." He knelt to pet both of them and got licks in return.

Daniel came up next to him, hopping on one foot. "Are they gone?" he asked, holding Wes's shoulder. "I couldn't find my other shoe."

Wes smiled as he went to the shelter building, flooding the area with light. An engine roared to life on the road and a red truck took off, pulling a trailer behind it.

"Well, that answers some of our questions. They do want Raj, as well as the dogs. And they are into dogfighting." Wes put his hands on his hips, shaking with anger at the cruelty people were capable of.

"And we have a name. We don't know who this Russell is or if that's a first or last name, but it's something to go on. And of course we can place Yan at the scene of the crime. That should be enough for the police to pick him up." Daniel returned to the tent, emerged with his other shoe, and put it on as flashing lights and sirens approached.

"Yeah. Hopefully our friends in blue will have an idea who this Russell guy is." Wes got out of the way as the cars pulled into the drive. Red got out, followed by Carter.

"You guys all right? For a second it sounded like a war zone out here," Red asked, on alert.

"The dogs made quite a fuss and scared them off," Wes said. "But we heard them. They wanted the dogs to train for fighting and Raj for some kind of games."

Red nodded, the light catching his eyes. "Shit. I thought we'd put a stop to that business last year," he told Carter. "Some of the guys heard about live gladiatorial games on the radio. The perps tried to get a bear. They got busted."

"But now they're after the tiger," Daniel interjected. "*Our* tiger. And this guy Russell seems to be the leader."

The officers exchanged looks but didn't say anything more. Red took notes, and then they checked over the shelter and the door that Yan's guys had managed to open. Industrial-strength bolt cutters had made short work of the locks. Wes thought the police might dust for fingerprints, but they said the door was too rough.

Wes yawned now that the real excitement of the night was over. It was just after two in the morning, and he was having to force his eyes to stay open.

"Do you know who Russell is?" Daniel asked Carter, as Wes leaned against the shelter door with the dogs curling up near his feet. They usually followed him around pretty closely, but even they seemed to be exhausted.

"We have some leads," Carter answered. "His name has come up in conjunction with a number of other incidents in town. But we haven't been able to find the guy. Unfortunately, this is just another incident. And it seems your visitors are trying to get in his good graces."

"My ex was one of them—I recognized his voice. The last time I saw him, he told me he was staying with some new friends. Maybe it's these guys, or even this Russell. I'm not sure, but he's up to his eyeballs in whatever is going on." Daniel yawned, and Wes pushed away from the door.

The dogs in the shelter had settled down, with many of them going back to sleep, while others sat, watching the proceedings. Daniel followed the officers around, full of energy, while Wes listened. Finally Red and Carter finished up and got ready to leave. "It's not likely that they'll come back tonight, but we'll swing by here a few times, just to make sure everything stays quiet."

"Do you think you can find this Russel?" Daniel asked pointedly.

"Count on it," Red said firmly. "We want him— badly. And what you've told us may be the lead we've been looking for. But rest assured, the first thing we'll do is find Yan. Since you recognized him, we can get him for attempted robbery, at least. And who knows— maybe he'll lead us to Russell."

"But you haven't found Yan yet," Daniel pressed.

"We will," Carter said, echoing Red's confidence.

Unfortunately, Daniel didn't seem so sure.

"Thank you," Wes said gently, hoping they were right. "We appreciate you getting here so quickly. And we'll definitely call you if anything else happens. Let us know if there's anything else we can do. We want these guys off the street and behind bars. They were intending to steal our dogs to use as fighting fodder. And that's not something we can ever let happen."

He nodded to the police, then wandered through the shelter, passing out treats to each dog and shutting out the lights. He closed the doors and then went over to check on Raj, who blinked at him from the door of his den.

"Night," Wes told him softly. "You did good." He left the tiger to rest and led the dogs back into the tent. Daniel followed, and they slipped under the covers.

"We have to do more," Daniel said softly. "We need help." He lightly patted Wes's chest.

"What are you thinking?" Wes asked, his mind already running with ideas.

"Maybe Mark, one of the clients at the clinic, would have some ideas. He's former military, and he knows a lot of people in town. It couldn't hurt to talk to him and maybe a few of the clinic's other clients. They love their animals, and I'm pretty sure they would keep their ears to the ground if they thought they could help. I'll make a few phone calls in the morning. It might even be worth calling Hank. He's a police officer, and maybe there's something he can share with us—unofficially, of course. Stuff has to overlap, right?" Man, Daniel was going as mile a minute.

"This is just so wrong. Just thinking about it makes my blood boil. Somebody has to be able to do something about it."

Wes could feel the energy radiating off him. He knew Daniel was worked up, but he figured there was more to it than just tonight's adventure.

"I know you're worried about Yan," Wes said gently. Knowing Daniel's ex had been here, and that he'd partly been after the dogs as a way to get even with him, had to be unnerving. Almost as much as the fact that Wes's father had been right… in a way. These men *were* after Raj for some kind of gladiatorial games. He wasn't sure what made him angrier—the fact that those men had tried to steal *their* animals… or that his father had seen it first.

"I just want him out of my life," Daniel whispered into the darkness as Reverend and Buster moved around, trying to find a comfortable place. "I thought he really cared for me… but obviously I was just something for him to own and control. And he's still trying to do that."

Wes sighed, wishing he could argue, if only to make Daniel feel better. But Daniel was right. So instead, he slipped his arm around Daniel's chest and tugged him a little tighter to him. "I don't know what to tell you except that whatever Yan does is on him and not you. Okay?"

"But he's joined the people going after Raj and the dogs because of me," Daniel countered, his voice rough.

Wes propped up his head. "No. He's acting this way because he's a dick. End of story. For the longest time, I thought that if I was better and did everything right, my dad would stop beating me. Every time he hit me, I thought it was my fault. It took a long time for me to understand the truth—that his actions were a reflection of his character, not mine. It's the same thing here. Yan is doing what he's doing because he's a horrible person. It has nothing to do with you. And he's going to be the one to pays for what he's done. Hopefully soon." Wes held Daniel a little tighter. "Don't give him that kind of power."

Daniel sighed. "How do I not?" he asked. "What did you do to stop your father from having it?"

That brought Wes to a pause. "I don't know if I ever did anything, other than tell myself that he was responsible for his own actions. I also had Mom telling me that none of what happened was my fault. She said it over and over, and I'm going to tell you the same thing. This isn't on you. None of it is." He lay back down and closed his eyes, feeling stronger than he had in quite a while. His father showing up again had thrown him for a loop, but being there for Daniel—seeing that he was back where Wes had been some years ago and knowing he could help him—only made Wes feel more capable. He could cope with what was happening, and with his father and the baggage that came with him. And maybe he could help Daniel process those same lessons when it came to Yan.

"But what if he never goes away?" Daniel asked.

"I'm sure the police will catch up with him soon. But really, the only thing that's important is that Yan doesn't have a place inside you. He can be out there doing whatever he wants, but you have the power to wipe him and his influence out of your head. That's what really matters," Wes whispered into the darkness. "I know it's easier said than done, but it isn't impossible. Maybe we can do it together."

And just like that, Wes knew he wasn't alone. Daniel and his problems with Yan, and his with his father, weren't so different. And they *could* help each other—that alone was comforting. "Let's try to get some sleep, and maybe things will look better in the morning."

Daniel snuggled closer, and Wes closed his eyes. The dogs pressed against his legs, and Wes let fatigue take him to sleep.

"HOW DID everything go?" Mitchell asked when he, Beau, and Jessica returned early the following afternoon. "Was there any excitement?"

Wes looked at Daniel, who shared his hesitation, and then Daniel explained about their late-night visit and what they thought was going on. "They want Raj?" Beau asked. "Are you serious?"

Daniel nodded. "For some kind of games, like modern gladiator stuff. It sounds sick, but when we mentioned our suspicions about them wanting Raj, Wes's father showed us an article he'd read on the internet. It's an underground kind of thing." He used his phone to bring up what he'd found, and Mitchell paled as he read. Wes had had the exact same reaction when he'd first seen it, and Daniel had slapped the table and shaken with anger.

Finally Mitchell handed Daniel the phone back and steadied himself on the back of the chair.

"Anyway, they showed up last night, but we scared them off." Daniel hesitated. "I was as pissed off as you are. I hope it's okay, but I called a few of our clients, including Mark Halperin. He's going to keep an ear to the ground and will let us know if he hears anything. I also called Hank, the police officer who told us about Raj in the first place. He's going to keep his ears open too, and let us know if the police come up with anything."

"Why were you here at that hour?" Mitchell asked, narrowing his gaze. "Don't tell me you two suspected something like this might happen and you let Beau and me leave...." His eyes burned, and Beau placed a hand on his shoulder.

"Calm down. They were watching over the dogs and Raj. That's what counts," he said gently.

"We didn't want to spoil things for you," Wes answered as calmly as he could. "We know you'd been looking forward to this trip for a while. And it's not like we knew for sure that they'd show up. We were just ready if they did. We camped out behind the shelter and scared them off."

Mitchell's cheeks were red, and his gaze raked over them. "I'm grateful they didn't get any of the dogs or hurt Raj, but you two took one hell of a chance. What if they had been armed?"

Daniel nodded. "One of the men was Yan."

Mitchell gasped and glared at Beau for a second before returning his gaze to them. "I'm calling the police. They need to put a stop to this."

"Red and Carter came by last night when we called. They want to find these guys just as much as we do," Wes explained. "Daniel was on the phone to them as soon as we heard something, but they were already heading inside the shelter, and we couldn't let any of the dogs be taken. Our plan was to call the police and let them handle things, but events moved more quickly than we'd expected." It was the best explanation he could give. He slipped arm around Daniel's waist. If Mitchell was going to be angry, then he could direct his anger at him instead of Daniel.

"I'm just glad everyone is safe," Mitchell finally said. "But what are we going to do going forward? We can't guard the place twenty-four seven." He turned to Beau, his demeanor shifting in seconds. "What if they're armed next time? They could hurt you, or Jessica. And then there are the dogs and Raj to worry about."

Beau soothed Mitchell with a light touch. "I think the best thing for Raj is for you to find him a permanent placement soon. Explain to your contacts what's going on, and tell them that he needs to be moved as quickly as possible. He's a very valuable animal, and these people need to get off their butts and make decisions. Otherwise we'll just have to look farther afield."

Mitchell turned toward the tiger enclosure, and Wes saw longing pass over Mitchell's expression. Raj sat at the edge of the enclosure, looking at their little group, blinking occasionally. Wes couldn't look away. Something about the beast touched his soul, and Mitchell seemed to feel it as well. "I wish I could just let him go and be free. Take him back to the wild and release him in a jungle somewhere. I know that's a terrible idea and that he's been in captivity too long for it to be even remotely possible, but I just wish he could have the life he should have had, and not spend every day in a cage."

"Me too," Daniel said, moving closer. "But like you said, he'd never survive. At least in a zoo, he'd have a larger space to move around in, and maybe he could even find a mate. I know cats tend to be solitary, but Raj can't spend his entire life alone in a cage."

Mitchell nodded slowly. "I agree. Let me make some phone calls and see what I can do." He went inside the house, with Beau following behind him, holding Jessica's hand. She looked so cute in her overalls and red shirt, like a little farm girl.

"What are we going to do?" Daniel asked. Wes shrugged. "There's only one lead I can think of that could take us anywhere, and that's Yan. Since he doesn't seem to have a problem finding me, I think maybe we need to let him do just that. We can set a trap. And then, once we have him, we can get him to tell us what we want to know."

Wes put his hands on his hips. "How? With rubber hoses? He isn't going to talk to either of us."

"Maybe not. But if we find him, we'll call the police. They should be able to make him talk." Daniel cracked his knuckles. "Maybe they'll even let us rough him up a little?" He waggled his eyebrows, and Wes groaned slightly.

"You already did that, remember? But I think the police idea is a really good one. These guys are dangerous. Who the hell knows what they'll do if they're cornered?" He leaned in and kissed Daniel gently. "I just don't want anything to happen to you."

Daniel smiled. "We have to protect Raj and the dogs. What if they tried to take Reverend? They wanted him when they first came to the shelter. We can't just let that happen."

"I'm not saying that. But I don't want you going off on your ex and his new friends. We don't know what they're capable of. That's all I'm saying. And before we do anything, we should connect with Red and Carter so they're aware of what we're doing." He took a deep breath. "I think finding Yan is a good first step. But we have to be careful. Last time he had a knife. What if he's graduated to a gun?"

Daniel leaned against him. "That's why we have to do this together."

Wes wasn't too keen on using Daniel as bait, but he agreed it was the fastest way to find Yan. "What do you have in mind?"

"We know he's been watching my place. And he's probably still doing it. So why don't I go home for a while? You can follow me, but stay just a few minutes behind. Call Red and Carter and let them know to be ready. If Yan is still obsessing, then maybe he'll make another move. And if he does, you'll be there and so will the police. We can confront him together."

It seemed simple—maybe too simple—but Wes knew it was worth a shot, as long as he could stay as close to Daniel as possible. "Okay. I need to finish the feeding, and then we'll go shake the trees a little." He still wasn't sold on the idea, but it seemed to Wes that Daniel was determined to do this and that he'd probably do it regardless of what Wes said. So Wes would make sure he was there to watch Daniel's back. And what a lovely view that was anyway.

Wes finished up the morning rounds and made sure Raj had his breakfast. Daniel had already left before he was done, and Wes didn't want to be too far behind him. Once all the animals were seen to, he hurried to his mother's car and drove into town, then parked on the side street outside Daniel's place and headed up through the back door, using the key Daniel had given him. He paused outside the door and then knocked before going inside.

"Any sign of him?" Daniel asked, but Wes shook his head. "Me neither. I guess it's not going to be that easy."

Wes closed the door, and Daniel grabbed a cloth, wiped down the counters, and then began to dust, fluttering through the room like a hummingbird, looking out the windows whenever he came close to them.

"It's okay. You aren't alone," Wes told him, slipping his arms around him when he got close and tugging Daniel next to his body. "Just relax." Wes leaned in, nuzzling Daniel's neck. "You know, if you're really nervous, I know a way to calm you down…." He licked at Daniel's collarbone, and Daniel went stone still, arms hanging at his side, the duster eventually dropping to the floor.

"I like how you think," Daniel whispered.

"I know you do. So relax. Yan isn't going to get in here without us knowing. Remember, we're the predators now, not him. We're hoping he'll show up so we can get information. He can't sneak up on you, and I won't let him lay a hand on you either."

Daniel remained still. "You said something about getting me to relax." A door closed loudly in the building, and Daniel jumped, knocking Wes on the chin. "I'm sorry."

Wes ground his teeth a little. "Why don't we bring this to an end. Is there any of Yan's shit still here?"

Daniel shrugged. "I don't know. Maybe in the closet. Why?"

"Call him," Wes said. The answer to their problem was so simple, it was staring him right in the face. Why hadn't they thought of this earlier? "We know that Yan was at the shelter last night, but he doesn't know that we know. We never said his name. So call him and let him know that you still have some of his things. Tell him that he has an hour or they're going in a Goodwill drop box." Wes stepped back.

"He might just go for it."

"And if he does, we'll call the police and let them know what's going on. Maybe they can park out of sight and be here when Yan arrives. They'll get their man, and we might get some answers." He grinned, and Daniel hurried to the bedroom. He returned with a few articles of clothing and a leather coat.

"He always loved this thing. If he doesn't come to get it back, then some needy person is going to look really stylish and warm." Daniel draped the coat over the back of the sofa, then got his phone and called Yan.

"I knew you'd come crawling back," Yan said through the speaker.

"Please. I just called to tell you that I found some things of yours, including that leather coat you like so much." He smiled. "I'll be at the apartment for about an hour, and then I'm heading back into the clinic. If you want your stuff, come pick it up. Otherwise I'll donate the lot to charity." Daniel's voice was steady as a rock, even though tension rolled off him.

"I'm kind of busy," Yan said.

"Then I'll assume you don't want your things. That isn't a problem. If I get a receipt for the donation, I'll be sure to send it to you, care of 'Asshole of the Year,' through the Carlisle post office."

Yan growled. "Fine. I'll be there in an hour. It just might take me a little while to get there." Daniel ended the call, and Wes called the police department and asked to speak with Red or Carter.

"They're off duty right now," the man who answered the phone said. "Can I take a message?"

Wes huffed. "Yes. Please contact them and tell them that one of the men who broke into the shelter last night will be at this address in less than an hour. If they want him, they need to get over here." He told the officer the building number and then ended the call.

Maybe this wasn't such a good idea. He was tempted to put Yan's stuff in a box outside the door and leave.

He wanted this to end as badly as Daniel did, but if Yan showed up and they didn't have any backup....

He returned to Daniel, who was watching out the window. "Are they coming?"

"I don't know. Let's get Yan's stuff together. If they don't show, we can leave it out in the hall." His anxiety rose with each passing minute.

Daniel jumped when Wes's phone rang ten minutes later. He answered the unknown number. When he heard "This is Carter," Wes breathed a sigh of relief.

"It's Wes from last night. Yan is on his way over to Daniel's apartment to pick up some of his things. He'll be here in less than forty minutes, I'd guess." He shaved a little off the time in case Yan showed up early.

"I'll call Red and we'll get there as fast as we can." Wes finally allowed himself to breathe. Thank God they'd gotten the message. "We'll arrive in unmarked cars, and we'll call before we come up."

"Thank you," Wes said, then ended the call and returned to where Daniel continued watching out the window. The trap had been set. Now they just had to see if their prey took the bait.

WES STOOD at the back bedroom window, watching the parking lot, while Daniel remained in the living room. "Anything?" Daniel called.

He was about to say no when he noticed a silver Corolla pulling into the lot. Red got out and headed to the back of the building. Minutes later, another car took the last remaining spot.

"Yan is here," Wes said just as Red and Carter went inside. He opened the apartment door for them to enter, then closed it behind them.

"Yan just drove in," Wes explained to the officers. "What is he doing?" he asked Daniel.

Daniel's phone chimed, and he read the message out loud. "He's letting me know he's here," Daniel answered. "He's coming up." Daniel went to the door while Wes and the officers stood back, out of sight.

Rather than knock, Yan pounded on the door. Daniel opened it.

"Where's my stuff?" Yan demanded. "I have places I need to be."

Daniel shrugged and pulled open the door, motioning to the sofa. When Yan stepped fully into the room, Red and Carter charged over to apprehend Yan, while Daniel hurried over to where Wes was standing out of the way.

"Yannick Andersen? We've been looking for you." Red flashed his badge, while Carter went through the process of cuffing him before Yan could fully react. "You're under arrest for breaking into the West Side Shelter last night."

"I wasn't there," he argued as he struggled against the cuffs. "And you can't prove I was. I have friends who will prove I wasn't anywhere near any shelter last night or any night. Multiple people will attest to where I was."

Daniel turned to Wes, some of his confidence fading. Maybe this wasn't going to be as easy as they'd thought. "You mean the people who want the tiger?" Daniel asked. "Great. Why don't you call them? I'm sure the police would love to talk to all of them."

Yan paled, and Wes knew Daniel was onto something. "And maybe these 'witnesses' will even thank you for giving these officers their addresses and telephone numbers."

Damn, that was brilliant. Yan was as white as a sheet. "I'm not giving anyone anything."

"Then your alibi just went up in smoke." Daniel crossed his arms over his chest. "And for the record, you certainly were there. I heard you," he countered, stepping forward. "And somehow I really doubt your so-called friends are going to stick their noses out of their holes for you, especially now that the police are involved." Daniel certainly wasn't backing down, which pleased Wes no end. "And if I were you, I wouldn't lie to these officers. The charges are already piling up. There's attempted robbery. Then assault and battery. And, of course, you threatened me with a knife the last time you were here." Daniel put his hands on his hips, glaring at Yan.

Red searched Yan's pockets. "This knife?" he asked, holding it up, and Daniel nodded. "A switchblade. Those aren't legal."

"You little shit," Yan spat at Daniel.

"That's enough," Wes snapped, and Yan closed his mouth. "Why were you at the shelter last night? We heard you talking to your friends. And we know you wanted the dogs for fighting… and the tiger too. We heard everything. If and when you ever get out of jail, you should tell your friends that smart criminals keep their mouths shut when they're committing a crime. After all, someone might overhear." He stalked closer. "Who is Russell?"

"I don't have to tell you anything," Yan snapped.

"That's true, you don't." Wes smiled. "But you know, these good officers could leave the room and just happen to forget their handcuffs. Then who knows what Daniel and I could do to you? And nobody would see a thing."

Yan sputtered. "They can't do that." He turned to Red and Carter as though they'd save him.

"Sure they can. Since they don't like you any more than we do, I'm sure they'd be happy to let an abusive shit like you to get what's coming to him." Damn, Yan looked like he was going to pee his pants at any second. "I'm sure Daniel would enjoy the chance to give you back some of the hurt you heaped on him."

Yan's eyes filled with fear, and he backed away.

"Now tell us who Russell is and what he wants with the tiger." Wes was about done with Yan. He pulled his hand back as if to slap some sense into him, when in fact he had no intention of touching the slimeball. He was just hoping the threat was enough to get Yan to open up.

"Harold Russell. He has a place on B Street and some land out northwest of the borough. He arranges dogfights and other stuff like that." Yan's leg shook, and Wes held his gaze, not willing to give him an inch. "The problem is that he needs more dogs, and that shelter was full of them. You turned his guys away, and he was pissed. So we thought we'd get him what he needed."

"Are the guys you were with your new friends? The ones you told Daniel you were staying with?" Wes demanded, and Yan nodded.

"Some friends," Daniel said. "They get you in trouble, but now that you're on your way to jail, I bet they'll hole up like the rats they are and let you take all the heat."

Wes smiled. Daniel really seemed to be pushing all Yan's buttons.

"Names," Red snapped, and Yan gave them over without a moment's hesitation. Not that voice two and

voice three were important, but giving names only got
Yan in deeper. There was no way out for him now, and
the best part was, Yan knew it.

"What does Russell want with the tiger?"

Yan sighed. He obviously knew he was screwed.
"People were losing interest in dogfighting, and Russell
had read about other kinds of games being offered. So
he came up with the idea of having other animals fight.
Joey and Randy had seen the tiger, and Russell thought
that would be an attraction big enough to draw in some
real interest."

Bile rose in Wes's throat at the thought of what
they'd planned to do with Raj. Hell, he wanted to
smack Yan into the middle of next week, but he held
his temper.

"What sort of games?" Red asked. "Were these
with other animals or people?"

Yan shrugged. "Both, I guess. Russell thought the
tiger would be a huge draw. He had visions of a man-
against-beast sort of thing. The guy is a little crazy, but
he has power and money, and he wanted the tiger. It's
just sitting in that cage not doing anything anyway."

Daniel lunged forward and slapped Yan across the
cheek. "How dare you? That's another living creature.
He deserves better than to be part of your sport so some
asshole can make some money off him." Daniel's eyes
blazed with sheer hatred.

"You're just keeping him in a cage," Yan countered. "How are you any better?"

"He's being cared for, and Mitchell is finding him
a home in a zoo. He could even help save his species
from extinction. But all you want to do is put him in
a pit to fight. Do you have any idea what he's capable
of? He could rip you and half the people watching to

shreds. But you don't care. As long as Russell's happy." Daniel backed away. "You're pathetic." He turned and slowly went into the bedroom, where he closed the door with barely a sound.

Wes figured he and the police officers had heard enough. They got Yan to his feet, and Red walked him out of Daniel's apartment.

"Well, I'd say that any time we need someone to play the bad cop, we should call you," Carter said with a grin.

"I was hoping you'd pick up on what I was doing. The guy is basically a coward and a bully. I hoped that if I scared him enough, he'd roll over and tell us everything we wanted to know." Wes turned toward the bedroom. "Do you have enough to put this Russell out of business?"

Carter cleared his throat. "I hope so. At least we've got a place to start now. We'll interrogate Yan some more and see what additional information he can give us. Then we'll investigate further." He crossed his arms over his chest.

"And what about the other men who were with Yan? Will you pick them up too?" Wes knew this wasn't over. They had gotten the small fish, but the big one, the real troublemaker, was still out there. "The guys who were at the shelter last night weren't the same people who approached Mitchell."

"How do you know? It was dark last night," Carter asked.

"Because the men who came before were in a black truck, and the ones last night drove a red one. And their voices weren't the same. The first men had deep voices, but the guys last night had higher voices, and they were a lot more tentative. Yan and his friends were trying to impress this Russell, but I got the feeling that the other men knew their place. Heck, one of them might have been Russell himself. I don't know. Mitchell took a look them and kicked them off the property. He knew something wasn't right immediately. There's a chance that Yan actually knows enough to lead you to these people. But there's also the chance that he doesn't."

"You could be right," Carter agreed.

"Yan is a yutz, a wannabe to these guys. They wouldn't have shared anything with him that's really important."

"That's a good observation," Carter said. "I'm betting that the location they gave him is phony as well."

Wes nodded. "You'll go looking north and west, and the actual place will be far away from there. If my suspicions are correct, this is a real money-making enterprise, and Russell will have taken precautions. He's not going to let a guy like Yan jeopardize it."

Carter nodded slowly. "You seem to know a lot about this sort of thing."

Wes sighed. "My father was an alcoholic, and one of the things he loved to do when he drank was gamble… and hurt my mother and me when he lost, which he always did. He got very good at scouting out any sort of game of chance where he could lay down the grocery money or the mortgage payment in the hope of making a big score. Drinking was always the catalyst."

He swallowed, hating that he had to recall that time in his life. "No one is going to set up a dogfighting operation just to watch dogs fight. There's a lot of money involved, and the house always takes their cut. It'll be a major gambling setup." Wes had no idea where these fights really took place. He wished he had some piece of information that would lead the police there, but he didn't know. All he was sure of was that Yan's info wasn't reliable. Still, he supposed the police needed to check it out, just to rule out the possibility. "I really hope you can find it." That was the only way Raj and the other animals at the shelter would be safe.

"We will," Carter told him with a confident smile. Wes wondered if they taught them that expression at the police academy. He thanked him again, let Carter out, and closed the door.

Daniel wandered out of the bedroom, his face tilted toward the floor, and suddenly Wes realized something. With Yan out of commission, there was no need for Daniel to stay at the house any longer. But Wes didn't want him to move back into this cold, lonely apartment. He liked having him in the house. Daniel brought life to the place, and without any proof, he knew that just being around Daniel's energy helped his mom. But it was more than that. With Daniel there, Wes was happy… something he hadn't known could happen.

"I guess it's time, isn't it?" Daniel said as he looked around the apartment. "I'm going to need to figure some things out, but when the semester starts up again, I'll be able to get another roommate. Then, next fall, I'll go back to school and get my degree in veterinary medicine, the way I'd planned."

"You can do whatever you want, and you'll be great at it." It was true. Daniel was going to be an amazing vet wherever he decided to go to school. Maybe it was best if things ended quickly. Wes needed to figure out what he was going to do moving forward, and….

Daniel lifted his gaze, and Wes caught those amazing eyes, the flushed cheeks, and dammit, everything he wanted was right there.

"I suppose." There was no enthusiasm in Daniel's voice. For a second Wes wondered if that meant Daniel felt the same way he did.

But he had never been lucky enough to get everything he wanted. Hell, most of the time he'd been content to sit on the sidelines, watching while others got whatever they wanted. "I suppose now that Yan is gone, you should go back to your own life. This is a nice enough place, I guess. I can help you bring your things over from the house if you want."

He sure as hell wasn't going to stand in Daniel's way. It was probably time for them to go back to their real lives anyway. All good things had to end someday, right? He told himself that the most important thing was that Daniel was safe. Yan had been apprehended, and now Daniel could move on. Even if Wes had hoped that maybe Daniel wouldn't want to leave.

Chapter 13

DANIEL WASN'T sure what Wes wanted. He suddenly seemed distant. He turned toward the door as if he was anxious to get out of here. He didn't invite Daniel to return to the house with him other than to get his things, so Daniel figured that was it. He'd go back to Wes's, pack up his stuff, and come back here.

It wasn't like he was never going to see Wes again. But it seemed that whatever Daniel had thought was happening between them had all been in his mind. He and Wes had made love, and Daniel had thought that meant something. But the way Wes was talking about Daniel's future, it sounded like Wes didn't want to be a part of it.

"I'll lock up here and meet you at the house. I can get my stuff, and then Buster and I will be out of your hair." He couldn't help letting the hurt creep into his voice.

"I didn't mean it like that," Wes said. "Yan is in custody. That means you can go back to your life now. Things can go back to normal for you."

Daniel rolled his eyes dramatically. "Look at this place. Does it seem like I want to be back here alone?" He tilted his head to the side. "It's a shithole apartment, but it's the only thing I can afford. I was desperate enough to cover rent that I let an asshole like Yan into my life because I thought he loved me. Turns out I was just stupid enough to believe anything he told me. Maybe that's what's happening again. Maybe I wanted there to be something between us because you were a good guy and so different from my usual type. You listened to me and really paid attention to me." Daniel glared at Wes.

"What is it you want from me?" Wes asked softly.

Daniel shook his head. "I want *you*, ya fool. Sheesh. Sometimes you strong silent types just don't get it. Normal people, like me, we talk about what we're feeling. And I want you, Wes. You make me feel special. I don't want to go back to my boring old life. I want… I don't know… evenings outside looking at the stars, and nights spent steaming up the inside of a tent that is way too small for two men and two dogs, but yet we somehow made it feel like it was the most special place there was. I want a house with enough room for at least another dog. Who knows, maybe even a cat."

Wes shook his head, growling as he drew closer. "No housecats. I'm allergic to them. But the rest of that…."

"What?" Daniel asked as he closed the distance between them.

"It sounds pretty good to me," Wes breathed, and Daniel let go of the tension that had threatened to make his head explode. "I didn't know what you wanted, and I wasn't going to try to influence your decision. That's something Yan would do. And I'm not like him."

"You're nothing like him. But you have to tell me what you want and how you feel. I can't read your mind." He wound his arms around Wes's neck. "So you have to tell me. I know you have a lot going on in that head of yours, with your mom, trying to figure out what you want to do, taking care of the shelter, and me." He smiled. "But it doesn't hurt to open up and let me in on what you're thinking now and then."

Wes closed his arms around Daniel's waist. "Well, I was thinking that you could come back to the house and we could make sure that Reverend and Buster haven't driven my mom crazy. And then maybe once she takes a nap, you and I could have a little quiet time of our own."

Daniel closed the distance between their lips. "That sounds about perfect to me. And after we do all that, then I think we need to meet with your father again."

Wes stilled and pulled back. "What's he got to do with this?" Daniel could feel Wes's hackles rising.

"Calm down. I'm not saying we should all be buddy-buddy or anything. But… like it or not, your dad is the closest connection we have to the seedy underbelly of Carlisle." Daniel snickered. "I never really thought of this town as having one of those, but I guess it does. Anyway, I think your father knows a lot more about it than he's told us." He kissed Wes, who squeezed him back tightly, and Daniel almost forgot his train of thought.

"You know, talking about my father while you're trying to get things going isn't the smartest thing you've ever done," Wes said.

"I know. But my mind is going in a lot of directions too. I want all the things I said, and I want to make sure that the shelter is safe, and that Raj ends up somewhere safe and not with people who will just use him…." Daniel shook at the thought of something bad happening to Raj. But he knew he needed to gather his thoughts and get them all going in one direction, especially with Wes holding him like this.

"Okay. Step one, let's lock up and go back to the house. Step two, let's take advantage of mom's afternoon nap and *not* get some sleep ourselves…. Then, step three, we can see about meeting my father to talk about your seedy underbelly that's become so fascinating all of a sudden."

"It's not *my* seedy underbelly. It's the town's, and I didn't even know it was there. But now that I think about it, I was probably living with part of it." Still, Daniel smiled, because if Wes could tap into some humor, he figured that was a good sign. "Maybe Hank can help us. I knew him in college, so your dad isn't likely to recognize him." Hank wouldn't be around in an official capacity, but still, they'd have some backup.

Wes didn't release him. "Is there anything you need here?"

"I've got everything I want," Daniel said gently, and the two of them began to sway back and forth. The movement was small, but it was just enough that it reminded him of dancing, maybe to some sort of intrinsic rhythm from deep inside them. Daniel closed his eyes and went with whatever was happening between them.

He was content—heck, he was more than that. He felt safe, warm, happy. All those words came to mind as Wes held him, and Daniel didn't want it to end. He refused to let any comparison to the way he'd felt with Yan enter his mind. Daniel knew he had done too much of that, given Yan way too much power over his thoughts and actions. But now it was up to him to get Yan out of his mind, and his life, for good.

Daniel sighed and took a deep breath, inhaling Wes's amazingly earthy scent, letting it take control of his senses. With his eyes closed, the aroma grew even more intense, and he mentally followed it, letting it settle into his memory so it would be always be a part of him.

"Wes," Daniel said quietly.

"Ummm-hmmmm," Wes hummed softly into his ear.

"I think maybe it's time for us to leave and start on step two." They either had to get out of here now, or Daniel was going to drag Wes into his bedroom. And while they would have privacy, he didn't want to bring Wes into the bed he had shared with Yan. That just didn't feel right, and he didn't want to taint what he had with Wes. And he *really* didn't want to think about the fact that Yan had cheated on him in that bed.

Daniel swore under his breath and tensed. He was doing it again—bringing Yan into his thoughts when he was happy with Wes.

Wes stepped back, his eyes filling with heat. "I know exactly what you mean, and I...." He swallowed, lowering his gaze slightly. "I'm not going to make love to you here. That would just be wrong." His voice grew rough and gravelly, sending a thrill racing through Daniel. He was more than happy with that.

"I'll lock up the apartment and meet you at the house." Daniel swallowed hard, still standing where he was, holding Wes. He had no intention of moving away.

Wes chuckled. "If we're going to move, then you have to let me go."

Daniel didn't budge. "Nope. Don't want to." He kept his eyes closed until Wes shifted. Then Daniel finally moved away, missing Wes's heat immediately.

Even though it was summer and warm outside, Daniel felt cold when he left the building behind Wes, even though the sun beat down on him. Wes was his own personal heat source. Still, Daniel sighed, watching Wes as he strode quickly to his mother's car, those old jeans hugging him in all the right places. Damn, Wes was a stunning man. Daniel had noticed before, but something was different now. It took Daniel a second to catch it, but it had been there. Wes had said he loved him. Well, in a roundabout way. He said that he wouldn't make love to him in a bed he'd shared with Yan.

How had Daniel missed that? He grinned as he pulled open the car door and slipped inside. Swallowing hard, he started the engine and drove out to the house, where he pulled into the drive and parked off to the side. It didn't look like Wes had arrived yet. He went inside.

Carol sat at the kitchen table, turning when he came in. "Wes is stopping at the store for me." She patted the chair next to hers, and Daniel sat down, Buster doing his little "pet me" dance around his legs. Daniel made sure there was room and lifted Buster onto his lap. "I wanted to talk to you."

"Okay," Daniel said softly as he met Carol's steely gaze. "You know, you and Wes have that same expression when you're determined about something. Or when you're being protective." He'd seen it each time Wes stood up for him.

"I know. My son has been through hell and back. We both have, and yet he still has a good heart. I don't quite know how that happened."

"Because of you?" Daniel asked.

Carol chuckled. "Don't blow smoke up my ass." Still, she offered him a small smile. "I want to know what you intend to do with my son."

A smartass crack about how she didn't really want to know what they did upstairs died on his lips. That wasn't going to help—not when he found himself staring into the eyes of a mama bear.

"I don't know," he answered honestly. "I mean...."

She nodded. "That's what I was afraid of." She leaned forward. "I like you, Daniel, but Wes has been through hell, first with his father and then with me. It looks like I'm going to beat cancer, which is an accomplishment in itself, but it scared the hell out of Wes. You can get through hell once in your life, but no one should have to go through it twice."

Daniel could agree with that. "What do you want from me?" he asked as she sipped from the cup of tea in front of her.

"I want you to know what you want as far as Wes is concerned. He deserves that." Carol set down her cup.

Daniel continued stroking Buster, who settled down on his lap. "Well, I want a million dollars and a mansion on the creek, but I'm not going to get that. I was being honest—I'm still figuring things out, and so is Wes. He still has baggage, and so do I." He was on a roll, but he stopped himself before he said something that he couldn't take back. He figured Carol ought to know what it was like trying to get out of a controlling relationship, but it wasn't his place to say anything. "I know you're his mother and you want to look out for him, but our relationship is ours, and the two of us will muddle through it, the same as everyone else." He smiled. "But I will tell you that I think it's good that he has you in his corner. Well, now both of us."

Carol seemed to digest what he'd told her and then nodded. "I suppose I can't ask for more than that."

"Nope. And if your next question is about how I feel about your son, then I'll give you the same sort of answer. I'll talk about that with him. I think he deserves to be the first to hear that sort of thing." He cocked his eyebrows as Carol sat back in her seat, nodding to herself.

"I think that's fair," Carol said as Wes pulled into the drive. Reverend raced to the door, his tail wagging a mile a minute. As soon as Wes opened it, he pushed forward, making sure he got attention before anyone else.

"Have you been giving Daniel the third degree?" Wes asked his mother.

"She and I were just talking, waiting for you to come home," Daniel said. "I should probably make us a late lunch." It was the least he could do.

"There's some pasta in there, as well as some stuff for sandwiches," Carol said before slowly getting up. "I'm going to lie down for a while."

"Are you feeling okay?" Wes asked right away, his worry showing in his voice.

"I'm fine. I've been up for hours, and I prepped some chicken wings for dinner tonight. I also got the lesson plans updated for one of my classes, and I have the others to finish. But I'm determined to return to the classroom in the fall. It may only be for a couple of classes, but I've sat around here for too danged long, and it's time I got back among the living." She patted Wes on the shoulder. "I think the same goes for you."

"Mom," Wes groaned, and Daniel turned away to hide his smile and let Wes be embarrassed on his own. "I'm fine."

"I think you are… now." She patted his shoulder again and left the room, with Reverend trotting off behind her.

Wes watched as the dog disappeared into the room she was using. "I think I've lost my dog."

"Nah. He just wants to make sure she's okay," Daniel said, and sure enough, ten minutes later, Reverend came back out and hurried up to Wes, who patted his head gently.

"You're a good boy, you know that?" Wes asked as Reverend soaked up the attention. Buster did the same on Daniel's lap.

"You know, the house is going to be quiet for a while," Daniel told Wes softly as he set Buster down. Wes stood as well, and Daniel extended his hand for Wes to take. Then he led the way up the stairs and closed his bedroom door, leaving the dogs outside. "Wes...."

"Yeah," Wes whispered before kissing him, his nimble fingers undoing the buttons on Daniel's shirt.

"Tell me what you did before," he whispered. "What you said at my apartment." He swallowed, hoping it wasn't just some throwaway line that Wes had used but not really meant. "Tell me why you wanted to wait until we were here."

Wes nuzzled the base of his neck, sending ripples of desire running through Daniel. "I'm not quite sure what it is you want me to say." The teasing in Wes's voice made Daniel growl. "Do you mean that I wanted to make love to you here?" Daniel nodded. "That I didn't want to be with you in the bed you shared with a yutz of epic proportions?" Once again Daniel nodded, and groaned as Wes's magic lips sent him halfway to heaven. "Is that what you meant?"

"Yes," Daniel whimpered. "That you want to be with me and you care about me." He needed to hear that so badly.

Wes stopped. "Of course I care for you. Don't you know how I feel?" He pulled back, his gaze deep and intense. "Oh wait, you don't, because I say things in my head and not out loud sometimes." Daniel's gaze met Wes's, Daniel's confusion lightening to desire. "I love you, Daniel. I know I have this weird habit of ruminating about things in my head and coming to conclusions without really telling other people. I seem to expect them to just know what I'm thinking. But I want more than that for you... for us." He stroked Daniel's cheek. "So I'm going to say it. I want there to be an us. I don't know what that will look like. Or where life will take us. But I want you and I to be together."

"I don't know those things either," Daniel told Wes. "But I know the moment I fell in love with you. It was when I first saw you sitting in Reverend's enclosure, just waiting him out, knowing there was something inside him that wanted more but needed time and reassurance to be able to break through his wall of hurt. I think that was a lot like me. Like you could feel what he felt. I needed someone to see that I was more than just someone who'd been hurt. That I was still worth something inside." He swallowed hard. "I know I sound sort of corny, but Yan took away a lot of what I thought made me *me*, you know?"

Wes nodded. "I do know. And it's hard to get that back."

"But you gave it to me. You were strong and supported me. I knew you had my back. We'd just met, and I almost instinctively knew I could trust you... and you didn't let me down." Daniel kissed him, tugging Wes down toward the bed. Daniel sat on the edge of the mattress, and Wes came right along with him.

"Sometimes I don't know who I really am," Wes admitted. Daniel stilled and looked into his deep eyes. "There are times when I think I know, and then at other times, it's like my father took all that away and I'm still figuring shit out. I hate that feeling. I want to know what to expect and what my place is in the world, but it always seems to be changing."

Daniel wrapped his arms around Wes's neck and drew him even nearer. "I want you to know that everyone feels that way, and not all of us had a dad like yours." He kissed him, and Wes spread his arms on either side of him, holding his body above Daniel's. "We all have to find our own place in this world. It isn't given to any of us. Even people who look like they have it all have to figure out the exact same stuff that we do. So if you want my advice, stop looking out here." He waved his hand around the room. "Instead, start looking in here." Daniel placed his hand in the center of Wes's chest and patted it a few times before slipping his hand under Wes's shirt.

"You're a real minx," Wes said, shivering. Daniel loved that he could make Wes react that way, because Wes often made him feel like he was completely out of control, in the best way possible.

"And you're a stud muffin," Daniel countered with what he hoped was his hottest smile.

"I am? Really?" Wes asked. "I never thought of myself that way." He raised his eyebrows as though he was considering the possibility.

"Yes, and sometimes how other people view us is what matters—especially when it comes to stud muffin-ness. If you call yourself that, you're conceited. But if I say that's what you are, then it's just hot." Daniel had had enough talking, and he put his lips to much better use. His hands got busy as well, stripping Wes out of his shirt and sliding over his strong chest. Daniel loved the flow of Wes's skin under his palms, and he groaned softly. Wes chuckled and then kissed him hard, pressing Daniel down into the mattress.

"You drive me wild," Wes whispered, and Daniel whimpered. He didn't think he had ever done anything like that before, and it was more than a little sexy. Just knowing he had that effect on Wes was empowering.

"And you make me hot. Sometimes I watch the way your jeans hug your legs."

Wes drew closer. "So you're a leg man. Is that it?"

"That and an ass man." Daniel slid his hands down Wes's back and gripped his buttcheeks through his jeans. "These are pretty amazing." He loved the firmness under his hands, and Wes clenched as Daniel kneaded. It was pretty amazing. Of course, if he could figure out how to get Wes's danged jeans off, it would be even better. But he already knew Wes's butt was baby smooth and soft.

Wes backed away and climbed off the bed. First he got rid of Daniel's shoes, and then the rest of his clothes, before stripping himself, sending fabric flying until he stood proud, erect, and intensely beautiful next to the bed. Daniel's mouth went dry and he swallowed hard. Wes crawled back onto the bed, sliding his hands up Daniel's legs, then over his hips and belly until Wes loomed over him, eyes blazing with heat that set Daniel on fire. Holy hell, he was amazing, and Daniel pulled him down, wrapping his legs around Wes's waist. He wanted as many points of contact as possible. And once Wes pressed them chest to chest, Daniel slowly began to rock.

"Sweetheart," Wes whispered. "You need to stop that or things are going to be over before they really get started." His eyes rolled, and Daniel stilled. "You have me going a mile a minute already, and…." He swallowed. "Just relax a little. I'm not going to leave you hanging," Wes told him gently, smoothing his hands down Daniel's sides, nibbling the base of his neck. God, he loved it when Wes did that. It really sent him into overdrive. "There's no need to rush."

Daniel cupped Wes's cheeks in his hands. "Are you kidding? Your mother is downstairs taking a nap. How long do you think that's going to last? Let alone the fact there are two dogs in this house, both of which are probably sitting outside the door at this very minute. It's only a matter of time before either they or your mother come calling. So if you want to show me you love me, you'll get on with it before I explode." He crushed their lips together, and Wes demonstrated very clearly that he could indeed get on with it, while blowing Daniel's mind so completely, he actually had to stop and remember how to breathe. He quivered under Wes's talented hands and looked deeply into his eyes, arching his back while Wes did things to him that Daniel had only dreamed of… and he had one hell of an imagination.

He arched his back, gasping when the two of them joined together. The stretch, the burn, the intense connection with Wes only grew by the moment.

Daniel stroked himself to the timing of Wes's movements, but Wes batted his hand away and replaced it with his own. Having his own hand on his cock was one thing, but feeling Wes's there was something completely different, something much more intense. Daniel knew what he liked, but Wes added anticipation and buildup, getting him to the edge and then backing him away only to push him once more. It was almost too much and yet completely delicious.

"Don't stop," Daniel breathed as he gazed up at Wes, who was covered in a sheen of sweat, skin glistening, mouth partway open, eyes wide as though this was the most amazing experience ever. For Daniel it was, and seeing that expression on Wes's face nearly sent him tumbling over the edge.

"Not gonna last," Wes groaned, and Daniel moaned softly, slipping his hand between his teeth to quell the urge to scream his passion to the ceiling.

"Fuck…," Daniel moaned out long and slow. "Then take me with you."

Wes squeezed tighter, connecting with that primal portion of Daniel's brain. All his neurons fired, and Daniel's release built to a crescendo that he could no longer control. He grabbed the bedding to hold himself in place, arched his back, clamped his eyes closed, and rode the passion for as long as he possibly could.

The clouds in his mind cleared slowly, and Daniel was grateful for that. The floaty time after sex when Wes held him and they lay together was pretty damned amazing. He didn't even try to move, and breathing seemed like a chore, he was so wrung out. "Good God," he managed to whisper. "That was…." He didn't have the energy for any more words than that.

"Yeah. Wow," Wes said, holding him tightly as a scratching came at the door.

Daniel groaned as Wes shifted, separating their bodies. He shivered and then lay still as Wes got a cloth from the bathroom across the hall and wiped them both up. Buster burst in and jumped up on the bed, staring at both of them, tail wagging. Then he jumped down and ran out of the room, only to come back again, bark, and leave.

"Your dog is a little nuts," Wes said as he slipped back into bed.

Buster returned, and Daniel got out of the bed and pulled on his pants and T-shirt. Buster ran in a circle before leaving the room and going downstairs to the quiet living room. He jumped up on the sofa and stood over Daniel's phone, which showed a missed call from Mitchell. "Thanks, buddy," he said, stroking Buster, who sat, tongue out, seemingly happy to have been of service.

Daniel went back upstairs and listened to Mitchell's generic message before returning his call. "What's up?"

"I got a call from Los Angeles, and they want Raj. They said that they are going to send a team next week to pick him up and transport him out there." Mitchell sounded relieved and sad at the same time.

"That's great." And Daniel really thought so, though he was going to miss the big cat. "They have space for him?"

"Apparently they have just finished enlarging their tiger enclosure. Their male passed away a few months ago, and they are hoping that Raj will be able to step in and become the pride of their tiger exhibit, as well as the father of a new round of kits." For such good news, even Mitchell seemed subdued.

"He's going to have a much larger home and be with other tigers. That will be good for him." Daniel sat on the side of the bed, taking Wes's hand. "That also means that we just need to keep him safe until they can come to pick him up." The threat to Raj was still out there, and the sooner the police found these crazy people who wanted a tiger for some kind of weird sporting games, the better. He only hoped Raj was moved before anything else happened.

"We will," Mitchell said, then ended the call.

Daniel slipped off his clothes and lay under the sheet next to Wes, who spooned right up to his back. Buster jumped up and did his circle thing before settling right in front of Daniel.

"This is nice," Daniel whispered as nails on the floor outside signaled another arrival, and seconds later, Reverend joined them on the bed, finding his place near Buster.

"The entire family is here," Wes said softly, and Daniel smiled. He liked the idea of them and their dogs as a family. Maybe it was too soon, but the idea felt right in his head, and for the first time, he didn't question it. Instead, he let himself be happy. In his experience, moments like this didn't last long, so he was determined to enjoy it. They still needed to talk to Wes's dad, but he put that out of his mind for now, not wanting anything to ruin this perfect moment.

Chapter 14

"I'M GOING to miss you," Wes said to Raj on the following Wednesday afternoon. There'd been no news on the fight front—the only thing he'd heard from the police was that they were still running down leads. It sounded to him like he'd been right and the information Yan thought he knew had been less than useful. Daniel had called his friend Hank, and he had agreed to help out as well. So he and Daniel were once again in the same situation—determined to keep Raj and the dogs safe.

Wes's call to his father had felt weird. While he phrased it as a request for information, in the back of his mind, he kept reminding himself not to put too much trust in the man.

They had all been extra vigilant, and grateful that there hadn't been any further signs of anyone watching the shelter. Maybe Yan's arrest had spooked them and they'd decided that taking Raj was too great a risk.

"Having a tiger talk?" Daniel asked as he approached. Raj sat up and yawned, probably to show off his impressive teeth, and then blinked at both of them.

"Just trying to figure out how to say goodbye. Mitchell said that the zoo people will be here Monday to pick him up. They're going to take him to Harrisburg, where a special plane will be waiting to whisk him away in full tiger style." Wes put an arm around Daniel, and they leaned against each other.

"I know he's going to be better off. But that doesn't mean I won't miss him," Daniel said.

Wes nodded his agreement and looked into Raj's eyes. He could only imagine what Raj had seen over his life, and Wes hoped that his future was going to be happy. All they needed to do was keep him safe until Monday.

"How was your day at the clinic?" Wes asked.

Daniel shrugged. "Sort of normal. No huge emergencies or anything. A few dogs came in sick, but thankfully Mitchell doesn't think it was parvo or anything, so that's good. How was your day? How's Carol?"

She had slept late that morning. "Mom went into the college for a few hours late this morning, and she really seems to be getting some energy back." Wes sniffed and then blinked. "You know I want it to be real, and yet I don't want to let myself truly believe it, in case it's not." He knew he was being dumb.

"Just let yourself be happy. Carol is strong, and she knows her body better than anyone." Daniel turned and leaned in to kiss him. Wes pushed his fingers through Daniel's soft hair and returned it.

"I know." He pulled away. It probably wasn't a good idea for them to be making out at Beau and Mitchell's place, even if they had taken Jessica swimming for a few hours. "I should get to work with the evening feeding and get the dogs and Raj settled for the night."

"I'll go home and have dinner ready when you get there." Daniel kissed him again. "Call if you need anything." He walked back out to his car as Wes headed inside the shelter, where twelve dogs all vied for his attention. They had found homes for a number of pups recently, and Mitchell said that he had more people scheduled to come in later in the week. Mitchell had told Wes more than once that nothing would make him happier than for the shelter to completely empty, but that wasn't likely. There were always dogs that needed help.

"Hey, guys. You all hungry?" he asked as he got out the food and started preparing bowls. The dogs all sat in their enclosures, eager to eat. A few were more tentative than others, and Wes took his time with them, hoping they could learn that they were going to be cared for and that he wasn't going to hurt them. Still, he was always careful and moved slowly so he didn't startle any of them.

"Isn't this a pretty picture?"

Wes stopped dead at the familiar voice from behind him. "What are you doing here?" he asked, turning to face his father. Wes didn't like this one bit. His heart beat fast in his chest. As far as he could remember, his father had never had any interest in dogs… or animals of any type. He hoped Daniel had seen him and called for help. Shit, this was not how he had wanted to meet his father.

"I came to see how you were doing. After our last conversation, I wondered if you were getting involved in things that you would be better off leaving alone." Shit, he should have known his paranoid father would see through him. His father's tone set his teeth on edge. The hint of warning in his voice was one he knew well. It had sometimes been the only thing he'd heard before his father began hitting him.

"I'm not, and it doesn't matter anymore. Whoever it is that wants Raj isn't going to get him. And next week he'll be gone. He's being sent to a zoo on the West Coast." Wes actually smiled at that. Raj would be out of harm's way, and hopefully whoever had put a target on the shelter's back would slink back under their rock.

"That's good for you," his father said, his tone neutral, but Wes recognized that look of avarice in those almost black eyes.

Wes set the food bowls in each enclosure, paying more attention to his father than to the dogs. He didn't trust him and never would. No matter how much his father might have thought he'd changed, the beast he'd been to Wes was still inside him, just waiting to come out. Alcohol had only stripped away the social veneer, revealing the real person underneath. But Wes had always known who his father really was. "I know you didn't come here just to see how I'm doing." He closed the final enclosure door and turned to his father. "What is it you really want?"

He stepped forward, and Wes smelled the old familiar scent of alcohol on his breath. He should have known his father would never change, but he hadn't seen through his father's bullshit the last time he'd met with him.

"What I want are your dogs and the damned tiger," he said with a grin. "I know you're the only one here right now. Your boyfriend just left, and in a minute, my friends will pull in and load up what we want." Malice rolled off him. "Do what I want, or I can always have my men go over to the house. They'll take care of your little boyfriend and my bitch ex-wife all at the same time." Any mask of civility was gone. All that remained was the base rottenness Wes had grown up with.

"You're Russell?" Wes asked. He shouldn't have been surprised.

"It's my middle name, remember?" He grinned again.

Wes was confused. "And you told us about the dogfighting ring? Why would you do that?"

His father laughed like some cartoon villain. "To throw suspicion off me and because we'll just relocate. We've done it before. The dogs are just convenient—the tiger is the real gravy."

Wes listened for tires outside but heard nothing.

"Now, are you doing to do what I want, or do I have to teach you a lesson the way I did when you were twelve?" His eyes grew even darker, but Wes stood his ground. "When I'm done with you, you know I'll take what I want here and then make sure your friends pay as well. So why don't you just make it easy on yourself—and them?"

Wes saw red. There was no way in hell he was going to let his father hurt his mother again—or Daniel. This man had done enough damage, and Wes was going to put a stop to it. "I'm not a kid any longer, and you can't intimidate me. So I suggest you cut your losses and go." He watched his father, reading him. When his father drew back and lunged, Wes stepped to the side and lashed out with all his force. "I learned how to box in college." He jabbed and caught his father in the nose, the crack of bone audible as blood gushed down his father's face. He punched again, jabbing his father hard in the solar plexus.

The man seemed to ignore the pain and attacked, but Wes danced to the side, hitting his father with an uppercut and then knocking his legs out from under him.

"You little piece of shit," his father roared, but Wes wasn't done. He slammed his foot into his father's chest and kept pressure on him. "Can't breathe...."

"Tough shit." He added more weight. "You terrorized me as a kid." He already had his phone out, and he messaged Daniel to tell him to get the police right away. "I lived in fear of you for years, and now I'm holding your life in my hands." He glared down. "I'm through with you. If you die, I'll simply tell the police it was self-defense. Then I'll explain who you are, and I'm sure when they search your shit, they'll find plenty. No one will remember you except as a slimy piece of shit. No one will shed a tear, least of all me." He gulped for breath, still glaring at his father, watching as he began to turn blue. All he had to do was hold still and his father would suffocate, and that would be the end of it. He'd never be able to hurt him again. But... he wasn't going to become what his father was. Wes pulled back, and his father inhaled deeply. Color returned to his lips and cheeks.

"I knew you wouldn't kill me," his father said once he managed to get some air. "You don't have the guts."

"You aren't worth the price." He could see that clearly now. His father wasn't even worth a second thought. It was over—he'd stood up to his tormentor, and now he could look himself square in the eye as the specter his father represented evaporated into the ether like fog before the sun. "The police are on their way," Wes said loudly as tires sounded in the drive. It was a bluff, but a hopeful one. "You and your friends are going to jail for a long time." He spoke firmly, and sirens sounded in the distance while more vehicle tires crunched in the drive.

Wes couldn't see, but he held his father in place. If his friends came in, he fully intended to make his father pay for bringing this kind of trouble here. He couldn't believe the asshole was behind this and that Wes had bought his sob story at the restaurant.

"Wes, it's me," Daniel called from outside. "I saw your father arrive and got help. We have the drive blocked, so his friends aren't getting their stupid-ass truck out. The police are on their way." The sirens grew louder and then stopped. It took about thirty seconds before a uniformed officer burst into the shelter.

"He attacked me," his father said right away.

"Oh, shut up." Wes smiled at Carter, thankful the officer was someone he knew. "This is Russell. He also happens to be my father. He and his friends showed up intending to take the dogs they wanted for their little fighting ring, as well as the tiger." He backed away and let Carter take over.

"But he attacked me," his father reiterated.

"My father swung first. He thought I was the weak kid he used to beat the hell out of," Wes explained. "I neutralized the threat."

Daniel hurried in and launched himself into Wes's arms. "You stood up to him," he said. "And I heard you in here. Is he really this Russell?"

"I am not," his father countered.

"Russell is his middle name," Wes told Daniel and Carter. "He thought that since I was alone, he could intimidate me into giving him what he wanted." Wes narrowed his gaze at his father, then shook his head. "He found out that wasn't a good idea."

"I see," Carter said and began leading his father away.

"You're going to just take his word for it?" he snapped.

"You'll get your day in court. But since you're at the shelter—a place you have no business being—I'd suggest you close your mouth and get into the car or else we'll add resisting arrest to the charges." Carter read Wes's father his rights before bundling him into the back of a police car. Then it was Wes's turn in the hot seat, answering questions from the officers, giving a statement, and then when Beau and Mitchell returned, he answered their questions as well.

"Your father really thought he could bully you into giving him the dogs and Raj?" Daniel asked. "Does he even know you? Did he ever?" His smile warmed Wes to the bone.

"When I was a kid, he could intimidate me, so he thought he could simply continue to do that." Wes sighed as he sat on Mitchell and Beau's sofa. "And here I'd hoped he'd changed. But I knew as soon as I saw him tonight that he was just the same or worse. The other day was all an act. Today I saw the real man, just like I remembered. And to think, I was nearly taken in."

Mitchell patted his leg once as Daniel took his hand. "I was the dumb one. I pushed you into meeting your father in the first place," Daniel said. "But he's gone now, and so are his associates. And I'm willing to bet that the police will find where he's been holding his dogfights."

Mitchell turned to Beau. "Which means I'm probably going to get a call about all the dogs they find."

"Are we going to take them?" Wes asked.

Mitchell shrugged. "I don't know. Most fighting dogs are too far gone to be retrained as pets. They've fought to survive, and they will think they have to do that even when it's no longer an issue. If they call, I'll have to take a look and see." Pain flashed in his eyes.

Jessica climbed into his lap. "It's okay, Papa," she said.

Mitchell hugged her. Just then, his phone rang and he answered it and listened. "That's a relief, thank you." He listened again. "I expected that you'd call…. Okay. Tomorrow morning will be fine." He listened some more and then hung up. "It's what we suspected. They found where the dogfights have been happening. There are half a dozen dogs there. They think some of them were stolen, and they're going to try to find their owners, while others are obvious fighters, probably strays. Tomorrow we'll go over to see which ones we can take."

"What about the gladiator arena?"

"It was a field with a chain-link fence around the edge." He shook his head. "There is no way they would have been able to contain Raj unless they kept him chained up." Mitchell sighed. "You did a great job keeping the dogs and Raj safe. Who knows what would have happened if they had gotten any of them."

Wes was glad the entire operation was out of commission. "There's something I don't understand." He met Daniel's gaze and slid an arm around him, happy that he was okay. The threats his father had made really brought home how much Daniel meant to him. The thought of his father hurting him had nearly made Wes go insane, and it was only his innate sense of decency, and knowing that Daniel was going to be safe, that had stopped him from taking his father out… permanently. Wes took a deep breath and let go of the last of his anger.

"What's that?" Daniel's eyes filled with warmth, making Wes lose his train of thought for a second.

"Why would he tell us about the gladiatorial games if he was the one behind it?" Wes asked. "Remember? He told us that bullshit story about the guy he knew in jail that day we had lunch with him. He mentioned the idea of gladiatorial games to us then." It puzzled him, because there was no way they would have thought of it otherwise.

Daniel shrugged.

"His ego?" Mitchell asked. "He knew what was going on and probably loved the idea of leading you on with the idea. Maybe if you'd been receptive, he might have enlisted your help. Instead, he got to tease you about the whole thing. Maybe that made him feel like a big man again."

Mitchell's explanation was as good as any, but Wes felt there was more to it. "I think he led us on to try to get some information from us. Dad always played on people's sympathies and used them to his own advantage. He probably told us just enough to keep us interested, hoping that we might contact him for more... and maybe provide him with the information he needed." He shook his head. "I don't know. I'll never truly know how he thinks. And frankly, probing the depths of his mind is an exercise in darkness and pain. That's a trip I've already been on and don't need to take again."

Daniel squeezed his hand. "Nope. We're going to figure out a brighter future ahead."

Wes knew that was true. The ropes tethering him to his painful past had finally been cut away, and he was free. He smiled back at Daniel, and the rest of the room faded into the background for a few moments. Daniel's lips moved, forming the words "I love you" as clearly as if he had shouted them from on high. Wes whispered the words back, his heart, mind, and soul free for the first time he could remember. And they all belonged to the man sitting next to him.

Jessica climbed down from Mitchell's lap and ran off to play, with Randi bounding right after her.

Daniel stood, still holding Wes's hand. "I think we should be going." They still had to explain to his mother what had happened, and that wasn't going to be pleasant.

"I'll see you in the morning," Wes said.

Mitchell nodded and got up to see them to the door. Wes stepped outside, with Daniel following. Hand in hand, they ambled over to where Raj sat at the edge of his enclosure, watching them.

"You're going to go to a new home soon," Daniel said, his voice a little scratchy. "There will be lady tigers, and you are going to make plenty of strong cubs." Wes wrapped an arm around Daniel, letting him do the talking for both of them. "We've loved having you here, but you'll have a better future where you're going."

Wes tugged Daniel closer as they watched Raj watch them, his tail flicking, head tilted slightly, as if he could almost understand what was being said.

"I think it's time for all of us to move forward." His future—their future, however it might look—lay out in front of them like a road just after the rain, glistening in the sunshine. "Are you ready?" Wes asked Daniel in a whisper.

"As long as the future includes, you... then yeah." He wound his arms around Daniel's neck and drew him into a kiss that quickly deepened as a sense of rightness and perfection washed over him. Wes lost himself in the kiss, but jumped as Raj growled loudly. Daniel snickered but didn't pull away as they turned to face Raj, who yawned and blinked at both of them.

"Maybe he's feeling left out," Daniel offered.

Wes shrugged. "I'd prefer to think of it as his seal of approval." And who could argue with a tiger?

Epilogue

DANIEL MADE the last trip from the garage to the small U-Haul he and Wes had rented. It was packed to the gills with everything he and Wes owned. He had let his apartment go a little less than a month ago, and Carol had allowed him to move his things into her garage—not that there was all that much. He'd sold most of his things or given them to Goodwill. After all, that was where he had purchased a lot of the things anyway. Still, it had been a tight fit, involving a real-life game of Tetris in order to get everything inside. He pulled the overhead door closed and latched it.

"I have these last few boxes," Wes said as he came out of the house.

"You'll have to put them in the back seat of the car, if you can find room." The plan was for him to drive his car and for Wes to drive the truck. They'd return it at the U-Haul in State College once they'd unloaded it at their apartment.

Wes got the boxes in and the back door closed. "When are we leaving?"

Daniel had gone over this a couple of times, but with all the excitement and activity, Wes must have forgotten.

"Your mom is at the college getting her office ready." He checked the time on his phone. "She should be back in an hour. We can't leave until we've had a chance to say goodbye to her." It was because of Carol that things had worked out the way they had. She knew a number of people at Penn State and had made a few phone calls. Although Daniel had planned to work another year and save money before going to grad school, she'd had other ideas. Carol had not only been able to get Daniel considered for the veterinary program this year, but because of his grades and experience with Mitchell, he'd gotten a teaching assistant position with one of the professors—which meant that a good share of his initial graduate pre-veterinary school tuition was covered. That made the offer of a position in the class too good to pass up.

"I know. I'm just excited to get there and get settled." Wes had a job waiting for him with the English department, working with one of the professors while he got his master's degree. He had decided that he was going to follow in his mother's footsteps, get his PhD, and eventually teach at the college level.

"We'll get there before five without much worry. Just relax." He moved into Wes's arms. "Where are the dogs?"

"They're in the house." He turned, and Daniel followed his gaze to where they both peered out the side window. Both Reverend and Buster had been following them around every time they went anywhere inside the house. They were pretty afraid that they were going to be left, but that wasn't going to happen. Their new house allowed pets, and they fully intended to bring their entire family along with them.

Beau's car pulled into the drive and stopped in front of the truck. "We were afraid you might have gone already." He got Jessica out of her car seat and smiled as he approached.

"I have something to show you," Mitchell said once he got out of the car as well. He fidgeted with his iPad and then turned it around the show them the picture. "That's Raj, of course, and the female is Shira. She's pregnant and expecting a litter of cubs in about six to eight weeks." Mitchell beamed. "Raj is going to be a father. The keepers say he's been amazing, and they are getting calls from other breeding programs for him."

"He was always special," Wes said, looking at the picture of Shira, with Raj perched on a ledge above her as if he was standing guard.

Mitchell nodded. "The keepers said that the cubs are healthy so far, and they think there are four of them."

"That's awesome," Daniel said.

"It is. We did something pretty cool. We took a chance when we took him in, but it really worked out." Mitchell closed the iPad and stepped forward, hugging Wes and then him. "We're going to miss both of you." He sounded choked up, and Daniel felt a bit of that himself.

"We'll miss all of you." He grinned at Jessica. "And you too, little miss. You be good for your daddies." She giggled and went to him for a hug. Then he passed her back to her daddy, and she settled right in where she belonged, in Beau's arms. "It's going to be hard to leave. I only came to this town for college, but it feels like home, and I met so many people here that…." He found it difficult to talk.

"We know." Mitchell patted his shoulder. "But you'll be back, and you'll always have a place here. And when you're ready, the clinic will be here for you. So go out there and take the world by storm." His eyes seemed wet, and Daniel swallowed hard. "You have to explore the world and see what's out there before you can truly appreciate what you have back home." He hugged Daniel again and then hurried back to the truck.

"Saying goodbye is always hard for him," Beau said gently. "There are times when I swear he's going to decide to keep every dog in the shelter." He hugged them both, and Jessica waved goodbye as they headed back to the car. He waved as they backed out of the drive, and Wes slipped his arm around Daniel's waist.

"You know, he's right," Wes whispered. "We have to see the world and try to make our dreams come true. You're going to be an amazing vet, and all the animals you care for are going to be healthier because of it. And I've decided that I'm not just going to study and teach literature, but write it as well. I want my books to be centered around animals and their plight." He pulled Daniel closer. Wes kissed him gently, and Daniel slipped his arms around Wes's neck. "I do love you so much. You helped me find a future I never thought possible."

Daniel grinned. "And you... well, you just make me happy. What more can I say?" He kissed Wes and probably would have continued if a throat clearing nearby hadn't intruded. He'd been so caught up in Wes he hadn't realized Carol had come home.

"I think the two of you need to be saying your goodbyes and getting on the road before the neighbors decide to turn the hose on you." She smiled, and Wes hugged her. Daniel did the same. Carol had become very important to him. "That's very sweet, but you need to get yourselves going, and those dogs are going to go through that window if you make the poor things wait any longer." She chuckled, and when Wes opened the back door, the dogs raced out and jumped into the car.

Daniel got Buster buckled in, and Wes did the same with Reverend. Both of them looked as excited as Daniel felt.

"You boys call me when you get there," Carol said, and then she stepped back as Wes climbed into the driver's seat and Daniel got into the car.

They pulled out of the drive and headed off, the sunny day as bright as their future.

Keep reading for an excerpt from
Rescue Me
by Andrew Grey.

Chapter 1

"OKAY, GUYS, I'm coming," Mitchell called as he opened the door to what had once been the low barn of the family farm. Few things made him happier than the barks and cries that started when he slid the door open first thing in the morning. "Everyone is going to get brekkie and no one will be left out, I promise," he said to calm the rabble, but it had no effect. He slid the door closed, smiled, and opened two of the cages so the dogs could run around his legs as he went to start preparing the food. They jumped around him, tails wagging. Come play with us. Mitchell scratched their heads and got to work, the dogs occupying themselves until he set down the bowls. They both attacked their food, eating and drinking, happy dogs. And Mitchell loved all fifteen of them.

Once Bowser and Bruno were fed, he let the two young labs out into a play yard and went about feeding the others. Those he could, he put with the labs so they could run and play. The newer arrivals he kept isolated in case of disease. And there were a few, like Jasper, who didn't get along well with other dogs. He fed him separately but paid him just as much attention as he did the others. These boys and girls were like his family.

"Knock, knock," a deep voice said from the doorway.

"Careful," Mitchell called back to the stranger. "Don't let any of them out." He believed in letting the dogs run and play as much as possible. He scooped up Randi before she could make a break for it. She was a little Chihuahua mix, lightning fast, and loved to try to make a run for it. He soothed her with pets as the door opened slowly and a man of about forty, in tan pants and a blue shirt and carrying a clipboard, stepped inside. He closed the door behind him.

"Well…," he said as he looked around. "What have we here?"

"I need to finish feeding," Mitchell said. He put a bowl out for the final dog and then put the old St. Bernard into one of the runs so he could either get some exercise or, more likely, take a nap. "What can I help you with?"

The man sighed. "There's been a complaint about the barking."

"I see. Let me guess—from the people who moved in over there." He pointed toward the now butter-yellow house on the other side of his. "They moved in two months ago and have called me three times because of the dogs. I've been running this shelter here for four years now. I was here first and I'm not going to stop." He put his hands on his hips.

"They apparently have a baby and—"

"Then they should have thought of that before buying the place," Mitchell interrupted. "I have fifteen dogs—" He stopped. "Maybe you should start by telling me who you are?"

"Clark Fenner. I'm with codes compliance at Carlisle Borough. We received a complaint about barking, and they claimed that the dogs were left unattended for long hours, that they weren't being fed properly, and that you had fighting dogs."

"Mitchell Brannigan, and my dogs are all well cared for. They're fed and well exercised. And I have a few former fighting dogs." He took Clark over to one of the runs. "This is Bosco. He was rescued a few weeks ago from a place in Lancaster. Bosco was injured badly in a dog fight. The police over there raided the place, and one of them called me. I picked him up and brought him here. Bosco is a good dog when people are around, but he's aggressive with other dogs. I keep him isolated from the others and am working with him. He may never be comfortable around other dogs, but I'm hoping to help him to behave better so he can be adopted out. Right now I'm near the cap of what I can handle, but I have three dogs being adopted out today and two more couples coming in tomorrow."

Clark narrowed his gaze. "How do you make money at this?" he asked.

"I don't. This is a nonprofit." Mitchell continued petting Randi; she calmed him down. He had considered adopting her himself. But then, he wanted to do that with all the dogs, and he'd long ago told himself that he needed to keep a distance or else his house would be as full as the shelter. "I'm also a veterinarian, and my practice is a mile up the road. I have regular office hours, and during those times, the dogs are in their cages. I know they bark sometimes, but it's a fact of life. These dogs are good dogs, and they are cared for. All have their shots, and I would never allow any of my dogs to be abused in any way, least of all used for fighting."

Clark's expression softened. "I see." He looked around once more. "I wasn't informed of that." He peered into some of the cages and then looked out into the yard at the runs where the dogs were playing. "Dang, that one's a beauty." He stopped in the doorway.

"Rex… yeah, he is. His family got him as a pup and thought they could handle taking care of him. He's a giant schnauzer and weighs about seventy-five pounds." Mitchell opened the door to the run. "Come here, Rex," he said gently, and the large black dog approached and nuzzled right in for pets. "He was too much once they had a baby, so I took him." Clark stroked him. "He's wonderful and incredibly affectionate. Rex has been with me for almost six months now."

"How long do you keep them?" Clark asked.

Mitchell stared, tensing. "Until they're adopted. I don't put dogs down here for any reason other than illness. There is no such thing as a bad dog, just bad pet parents. Rex will be with me until he finds a home. They all will."

Rex approached Clark, and soon he sat right next to him as Clark petted and talked to him softly.

"I have a fenced-in backyard in town, and my wife spends a lot of time alone during the day while I'm working. Would it be okay if I brought her over later to meet Rex here?" He knelt down, and Rex practically put his head on Clark's shoulder, soaking in the attention.

Mitchell knew that look, and he turned away, smiling, because he knew Rex had likely found a home. That spark when a dog and person clicked was definitely there.

"That would be great. Please take some pictures of your yard, and I'll have some paperwork for you to fill out when you come back, and I can explain the adoption fees. I want to make sure you understand how to care for him. Of course he's had all his shots, and I have his records. If you adopt one of my dogs, then I give a discount on all vet care for the rest of the dog's life." He was going to be sad to see Rex go, but if it was to a good home, then that was the best thing.

Clark smiled brightly. "Thank you." He continued petting Rex, and Mitchell had a pretty good idea that he was falling in love. That sort of thing was a lot easier with dogs than it was with people. Dogs gave love no matter what, and they did it without regard to looks or taste or whether you happened to snore. And dogs certainly had a sense about people… something Mitchell sorely wished he could borrow. His history of relationships left a lot to be desired, and he much preferred the company of animals to that of people. At least he understood their motives.

"I'll be back with my wife. I'm sure she's going to be as taken with him as I am." Clark took a few pictures and sent them off, and his phone chimed a few seconds later. Clark rolled his eyes and messaged back. "She says she's wanted a dog for years and was waiting for me to come around. So I guess if you'll hold him for us, we'll come around later and get him."

"Wonderful," Mitchell said. He went to the office and pulled out the papers he required, along with a list of supplies he recommended for a dog like Rex. "Here is the information I need filled out. Also a list of supplies and the kind of food he's on. When you come back, I'll talk to both of you about his care." This was a banner day as far as he was concerned. "I take it there's no problem with the shelter."

"None. I'll address the complaint at the borough and close it as baseless. I would suggest you might want to see if you can talk to your neighbor. Try to get to know them a little. Maybe if they understand what you're doing, you can patch things up."

What Clark said made sense. Mitchell needed to figure out how to smooth things over with his neighbor.

MITCHELL CLOSED the clinic and then stopped at the shelter to feed all of the dogs and get them in for the night. As usual, he was greeted with yips, barks, and wagging tails. He started the process for evening feeding as a car pulled into the drive, followed by another, and then a third. Mitchell greeted his visitors and reviewed the care of their new pets with each of them before waving goodbye as three of his dogs found new homes. Once the shelter was quiet again, he finished feeding and brushed Rex so he looked good when Clark and his wife stopped by. He was truly sad to see him go, but the way Rex perked up when he heard Clark's voice, and then the excitement when his wife saw him, sent a jolt of joy racing through his heart.

"He's beautiful."

"Isn't he?" Mitchell said as he led Rex out on a leash. He went right up to her and nuzzled in, and she began petting him like Rex was a long-lost friend.

"We'll take him, of course," she said. "Clark has all the paperwork done, and we have the supplies in the trunk. And because he's so big, we got him a raised water and food bowl as well as a bunch of toys." She took the leash, and Rex practically pranced as she walked him around the yard outside the shelter. "Is there anything else we need to do?" she asked brightly.

"I don't think so. Not right now. Just make sure he has a bed or he'll want to sleep on yours, and Rex will take up most of the space." He smiled, and they nodded. They both shook his hand before they left the shelter. Mitchell watched them go and went back inside, closed up the shelter for the night, and headed out to the house.

Mitchell figured he could eat once he got back, so he packed up the cookies that one of his patients had brought to the clinic, checked himself in the mirror, and then headed up the street to the neighbors' for a visit.

He wasn't quite sure what to expect. He knew someone was home. He'd seen a man out in the yard a few times, but mostly the place seemed buttoned up and quiet. Still, he strolled along the road and then up the drive and the walk, to the front door, where he knocked softly. He heard movement inside and was about to ring the bell when the door opened and a haggard man in his midthirties, the same as Mitchell, stared at him. A baby wailed on his shoulder. "I'm sorry, did I wake the baby?"

The man shook his head. His hair was all askew and his brown eyes half-lidded, lips drawn into a line, and his skin a little sallow, like he was too tired to move. Still, he was handsome under all the dishevelment, with a granite jaw and high cheekbones. "No. She's been fussy all night." Mitchell held up the plate of cookies, and the man pushed open the door. "Come on in. I hope she'll wear herself out soon." He patted her back, and the little thing fussed and sniffled.

"Is she sick?"

"I don't know. She doesn't have a fever, but she keeps pulling up her legs and cries like crazy. The doctor says she's losing weight, so I feed her whenever she's hungry, but the little thing doesn't have an appetite." He was clearly worried sick and at his wits' end. "I'm Beau, by the way. Beau Pfister."

"Mitchell Brannigan. I have the farm next to you." He wasn't going to hide who he was. That wasn't the way to start things off with a neighbor.

"The one with the dogs? How many do you have over there, anyway? I just get her down to sleep and they bark, and she wakes… it's…."

"At the moment, twelve. I adopted out three today. I run a shelter out of the old barn. I insulated it and made a good home for them in there. Basically, I rescue the dogs that no one else seems to want and find them good homes. I'm also the vet with the office up the road."

The little girl took the opportunity to wail once again and then farted, except she did more than that.

"Excuse me, I need to change her." Beau made a stink face. "I'll be right back. Have a seat if you like." He raced away.

Mitchell set the cookies on the table and automatically folded the blankets strewn over one end of the sofa. Then he sat down to wait. At least the baby had stopped fussing.

"Sorry," Beau said when he came back, a quiet baby in his arms.

"No need. I understand. The hard part is that she can't tell you what's wrong." Mitchell understood that. His professional life would be so much easier if he were Dr. Doolittle. "Can I ask what she's eating?"

"Formula. Her mother, Amy, is… was my best friend, and she named me Jessica's guardian in case something happened." He leaned forward, holding his head in his hands. "How was I supposed to know some drunk driver would hit her on her way home from work?"

"I'm sorry. How long have you had Jessica?"

"Just over three weeks, I guess."

Mitchell sighed. "Why don't you show me what you're feeding her. Was she being breastfed prior to that?"

Beau hefted himself out of the chair. "No. Amy couldn't, so Jessica was always on formula, and I got the same kind." He brought back two containers. One was empty and the other half full. "I kept this one so I'd know what to get."

Mitchell saw the issue almost immediately. "This is what she was eating before?" he asked, just to be sure, and Beau nodded. "Then it's the formula. Get this exact same kind in the orange container. This is lactose-free. I bet little Jessica has a milk sensitivity and the lactose is upsetting her tummy. Does she always have explosive diapers?"

Beau nodded.

"That would explain it. Change her formula. I bet her appetite will come back when her tummy doesn't hurt, and her diaper changes won't be as messy."

"Are you sure?" Beau asked.

Mitchell shrugged. "I'm not a doctor, I'm a vet. But a lot of what goes into various creatures and people makes a huge difference in their lives and health." He showed Beau the label. "This is lactose-free, and what you're using isn't."

Beau sighed. "To tell you the truth, I'd give just about anything for her to sleep for a few hours. Maybe then I could do the dishes or just take a nap." He yawned and sat back in the chair. Mitchell was afraid Beau was going to drop off to sleep any second.

"Maybe I should go and let you rest. I just wanted to stop by and say hello." He didn't go into defusing the situation about the dogs. He didn't want to bring that up.

"I'm glad you stopped. It's been nice to talk to someone who can talk back." Beau half smiled. "And thank you for the cookies. It's been so long since I ate anything that didn't come out of the freezer and the microwave, I think I've forgotten what real food tastes like." He opened the door, and Mitchell got set to leave.

"Then why don't you and Jessica come over for dinner sometime? My cooking isn't gourmet, but most people find it edible, and a lot of what I cook I learned from my mother. If you want home cooking, I can manage that." He smiled.

"Are you sure?" Beau asked. "A lot of the time, Jessica gets fussy and I need to take care of her. I used to have a lot of friends, but most of them don't know what to make of me with her, so they call and stuff, but the nights we used to get together have turned into story time, diaper changes, and bottles. Even the ones who had kids, theirs are older now and they have their own lives." He shrugged. "But if you're serious, I'd be happy to come to dinner."

Mitchell stepped out into the late evening air. The last of the summer light was just fading as he turned toward home. "Stop by tomorrow. I usually get home about six, and I have to feed the dogs. So about seven will work."

"I'll see you then," Beau said and closed the door.

Mitchell headed for home, wondering what he was going to make for dinner tomorrow. At least he seemed to have patched things up with his handsome neighbor.

ANDREW GREY is the author of more than one hundred works of Contemporary Gay Romantic fiction. After twenty-seven years in corporate America, he has now settled down in Central Pennsylvania with his husband of more than twenty-five years, Dominic, and his laptop. An interesting ménage. Andrew grew up in western Michigan with a father who loved to tell stories and a mother who loved to read them. Since then he has lived throughout the country and traveled throughout the world. He is a recipient of the RWA Centennial Award, has a master's degree from the University of Wisconsin–Milwaukee, and now writes full-time. Andrew's hobbies include collecting antiques, gardening, and leaving his dirty dishes anywhere but in the sink (particularly when writing). He considers himself blessed with an accepting family, fantastic friends, and the world's most supportive and loving partner. Andrew currently lives in beautiful, historic Carlisle, Pennsylvania.

Email: andrewgrey@comcast.net
Website: www.andrewgreybooks.com

Follow me on BookBub

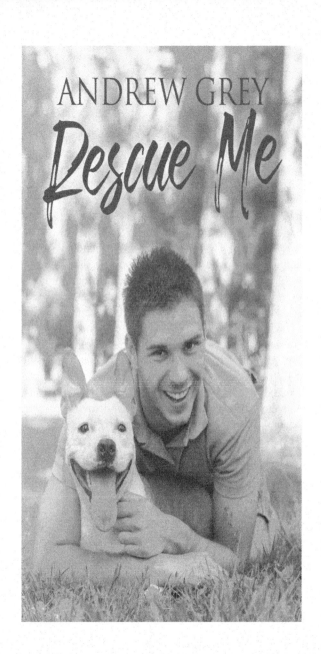

Everybody needs to be rescued sometime.

Veterinarian Mitchell Brannigan gets off to a rocky start with his new neighbor when someone calls the town to complain about the noise. Mitchell runs a shelter for rescue dogs, and dogs bark. But when he goes to make peace, he meets Beau Pfister and his fussy baby daughter, Jessica… and starts to fall in love.

Beau moved out to the country to get away from his abusive ex-husband, but raising an infant alone, with no support network, is lonely and exhausting. The last thing he expects is a helping hand from the neighbor whose dogs he complained about.

Mitchell understands what it's like to live in fear of your ex, and he's determined to help Beau move on. But when an unseen menace threatens the shelter and Beau, it becomes apparent that he hasn't dealt with his own demons.

With each other and a protective Chihuahua for support, Mitchell, Beau, and Jessica could make a perfect family. Mitchell won't let anything happen to them.

But who's going to rescue him?

www.dreamspinnerpress.com

First impressions are never what they seem.

LOST
AND
FOUND

ANDREW GREY

Rafe Carrera hasn't seen his Uncle Mack since he was a kid, so when he inherits his ranch, it throws him like a bucking horse. He's been on his own for a long time. Now suddenly everyone wants to be his friend… or at least get friendly enough to have a chance in buying the ranch.

Russell Banion's family may own a mega-ranch in Telluride, but Russell made his own way developing software. He misses his friend Mack, and purchasing the ranch will help him preserve Mack's legacy—and protect his own interests. It's a win-win. Besides, spending time with Rafe, trying to soften him up, isn't exactly a hardship. Soon Russell realizes he'll be more upset if Rafe does decide to leave.

But Rafe isn't sure he wants to sell. To others in the valley, his land is worth more than just dollars and cents, and they'll do anything to get it. With Russell's support, Rafe will have to decide if some things—like real friendship, neighborliness, and even love—mean more than money.

www.dreamspinnerpress.com

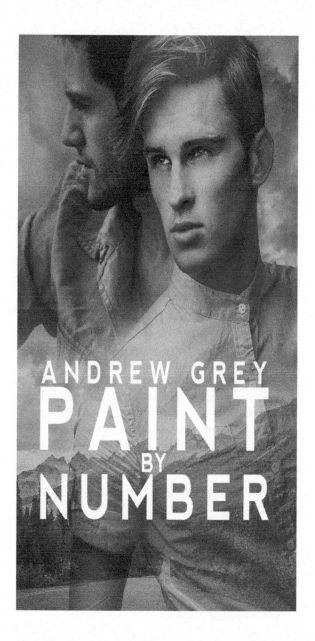

ANDREW GREY

PAINT
BY
NUMBER

Can the Northern Lights and a second-chance romance return inspiration to a struggling artist?

When New York painter Devon Starr gives up his vices, his muses depart along with them. Devon needs a change, but when his father's stroke brings him home to Alaska, the small town where he grew up isn't what he remembers.

Enrique Salazar remembers Devon well, and he makes it his personal mission to open Devon's eyes to the rugged beauty and possibilities all around them. The two men grow closer, and just as Devon begins to see what's always been there for him, they're called to stand against a mining company that threatens the very pristine nature that's helping them fall in love. The fight only strengthens their bond, but as the desire to pick up a paintbrush returns, Devon also feels the pull of the city.

A man trapped between two worlds, Devon can only follow where his heart leads him.

www.dreamspinnerpress.com

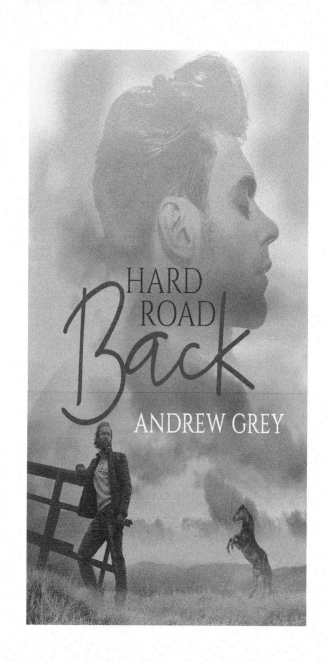

HARD ROAD
Back

ANDREW GREY

Rancher Martin Jamuson has a deep understanding of horses. He just wishes his instincts extended to his best friend, Scarborough Croughton, and the changes in their feelings toward each other. Martin may be the only friend Scarborough has in their small town, but Scarborough is a man of secrets, an outsider who's made his own way and believes he can only rely on himself when the chips are down. Still, when he needs help with a horse, he naturally comes to Martin.

As they work together, Martin becomes more determined than ever to show Scarborough he's someone he can trust… maybe someone he can love. Even if it risks their friendship, both men know the possibility for more between them deserves to be explored. But when Scarborough's past reemerges, it threatens his home, horses, career, and even their lives. If they hope to survive the road before them, they'll have to walk it together… and maybe make the leap from cautious friends to lovers along the way.

www.dreamspinnerpress.com

andrew grey

Catch

of a Lifetime

Some moments happen once in a lifetime, and you have to catch them and hold on tight.

Arty Reynolds chased his dream to Broadway, but after his father is injured, he must return to the small fishing community where he grew up, at least until his dad is back on his feet.

Jamie Wilson fled his family farm but failed to achieve real independence. Arty is hiring for a trip on the gulf, and it'll get Jamie one step closer to his goal.

Neither man plans to stay in Florida long-term, neither is looking for love, and they're both blown away by the passion that sparks between them. But on a fishing boat, there's little privacy to see where their feelings might lead. Passion builds like a storm until they reach land, where they also learn they share a common dream. The lives they both long for could line up perfectly, as long as they can weather the strain on their new romance when only one of them may get a chance at their dream.

www.dreamspinnerpress.com

FOR **MORE** OF THE **BEST GAY ROMANCE**

DREAMSPINNER PRESS

dreamspinnerpress.com